# dish #5

**Truth Without the Trimmings**

friends, cooking, eating, talking, life.

Grosset & Dunlap

# dish

**#5**

## Truth Without the Trimmings

riends, cooking, eating, talking, life.

By Diane Muldrow

Illustrated by Barbara Pollak

Grosset & Dunlap
New York

For Megan Bryant—D.M.

Text copyright © 2002 by Diane Muldrow. Illustrations copyright © 2002 by Barbara Pollak. All rights reserved. Published by Grosset & Dunlap, a division of Penguin Putnam Books for Young Readers, 345 Hudson Street, New York, NY, 10014. GROSSET & DUNLAP is a trademark of Penguin Putnam Inc. Published simultaneously in Canada. Printed in the U.S.A.

Library of Congress Cataloging-in-Publication Data is available.

ISBN 0-448-42871-7     A B C D E F G H I J

Molly Moore inhaled deeply. "Ah! Pizza!" she said. Her green eyes gazed hungrily down at the pie in front of her.

"I wonder if we could get their recipe," Amanda Moore said. Amanda was Molly's eleven-year-old identical twin. "What do you think, Molls? It's probably way different than the one we have. Would you go ask for it?"

Even though Amanda was in the same booth as Molly, she practically had to shout. The first Windsor Middle School basketball game of the season had just ended, and Pizza Roma was packed with noisy kids celebrating the team's win.

"Why don't you get it?" Molly asked.

"You're better at stuff like that," Amanda replied. That was true. Molly was the more outgoing of the twins. Amanda was more cautious.

Their friends Peichi Cheng and Natasha Ross slid into the booth with them.

"That game was *sooo* amazing!" Peichi said.

"It was awesome," Amanda agreed.

Molly suddenly stood. "The pizza chef just came out

of the kitchen. I'm going to go ask him for the recipe for their crust," she said. "Dish could make pizzas."

"Why bother?" asked Peichi. "I like the pizza crust recipe we already have."

Natasha pulled a gooey slice from the pie. "We need to make homey meals," she said. "Our clients want home cooking. If people want pizza like Pizza Roma, they can just call up and order it from them. They don't need Dish for that."

Dish was a cooking club that the girls had started. And now they spent a lot of time talking about food. A *lot* of time.

Actually, Dish was a combination club and business. The girls—or the Chef Girls, as they liked to call themselves—sold the food they made to the people in their Brooklyn, New York, neighborhood of Park Terrace. Most of the people who lived in Park Terrace were families, and many of the parents went off to work every day. Some of them worked in Brooklyn, but many took the subways into Manhattan. By the time they returned home at night, they were tired—often too tired to cook dinner. There were lots of places in Park Terrace where these weary parents could get take-out food, but none of them offered old-fashioned home-cooked meals. That's what Dish did—and they did it well.

Molly picked up her piece of pizza and began to eat. A glob of tomato sauce fell onto her sleeve.

"Oh no, Molls!" Amanda cried. "You spilled tomato sauce on your sweatshirt. Come on, let's go to the bathroom and see if we can wash it out."

Molly looked down at the stain. "Bummer," she said, but she kept eating. "I'm not worried about it. It'll come out in the wash." She clearly didn't want to get up and clean her sweatshirt in the bathroom. The girls were identical twins, but it was easy to tell them apart. Molly—whose real name was Amelia—liked sports and sporty clothing. She usually wore her dark hair in a high ponytail. And she didn't care much about the latest fashions or trends. Amanda read lots of magazines and was always in the know about the hottest styles. Today she was wearing a fuzzy blue turtleneck over embroidered flare jeans. Her dark hair was pulled back with a skinny headband that was covered in sparkling beads.

Just then, Connor Kelley, Justin McElroy, and Omar Kazdan stopped at the girls' table. They had been on their way to the counter for second helpings of pizza. "How cool was that game?" Justin said.

"Completely cool," Amanda agreed, smiling her brightest smile at him. In her opinion, Justin was the cutest, nicest boy she'd ever met. "The JV team really rocks," she added.

"The cheerleaders had some cool moves, too," said Connor.

"Ooh-ooh-ooh! Connor was staring at the

3

cheerleaders," Omar teased him. This was nothing new. Connor and Omar always goofed on each other. They'd done it the whole time they were in cooking class last summer with the girls.

Connor's cheeks turned red. "I mean it about the cheerleaders. That human pyramid they made was pretty amazing."

"It was," Molly agreed. Their friend, Shawn Jordan, was a cheerleader as well as a member of Dish. She'd stood in the middle of the human pyramid, helping to support the girls on the top. Molly had held her breath the whole time. She hoped Shawn wouldn't fall down under the weight and send the whole team tumbling. But Shawn stood steady and smiled confidently as the crowd cheered.

Of course it was totally like Shawn to stay calm. Everything about her—from her green cat's-eye glasses to her dark, curly hair and beautiful, mocha-colored skin—was cool.

"It's a bummer Shawn couldn't come out for pizza with us," Molly said.

"Why couldn't she?" Natasha asked.

"Her dad told her she had to come home right after the game," Molly explained. "She didn't say why."

"Wow! I hope everything's all right," Amanda said.

Omar's stomach grumbled loudly and he laughed. "Oops, sorry," he said, rubbing his middle. "I need more pizza!"

"See ya," Justin said to the girls as the boys continued on up to the pizza counter.

"Later," Peichi called after them. She turned her attention back to her friends. "I want to talk to you guys about something," she said.

"What's up?" Amanda asked.

"Some new people are moving in next door to my family tomorrow," she said.

"Have you met them?" Amanda asked. "It's always scary getting new neighbors. They could be great or horrible. You just don't know." The homes in Park Terrace stood in a row. Light came in from the front and the back windows, but all the sides of the homes butted up against one another.

"Do they have any kids?" Natasha asked.

"Yeah, maybe a gorgeous eleven-year-old son who needs someone to show him around the middle school," Amanda suggested hopefully.

"Sorry, no. My parents met them already. They said they were really nice and have one little kid," Peichi answered.

"Hey! You could make some baby-sitting bucks," Molly commented.

"Maybe," Peichi said. "Anyway, I was wondering if we could all get together tomorrow to cook a few meals for the family. They haven't really unpacked yet. My mom said it would be nice to welcome them to the neighborhood. What do you guys think?"

"It would definitely be a nice thing to do," Natasha agreed.

"And a good way for you to get to know them," Amanda added.

"Plus it's a great way to get a new customer," said Molly. "But we're not gonna charge them for this, right?"

"No, of course not," Peichi answered.

"What should we make?" Amanda asked.

"We could roast a chicken with herbs," Peichi suggested.

"While the chicken is cooking, we could bake some potatoes," Amanda said.

"Let's make a lasagna, too," Molly suggested. "Everybody loves a warm, gooey, yummy lasagna."

Peichi laughed. "We won't even have to put it in the freezer. It's been so cold out lately that by the time we bring it to their house it will freeze all on its own!"

"What do you think about putting sausage in a mac-and-cheese casserole?" Natasha asked. "I saw a recipe for it in a magazine."

Molly, Amanda, and Peichi shot her skeptical looks. "I don't know," Amanda said slowly. "It seems wrong somehow to mess with a classic like mac and cheese."

"Yeah, and don't forget that they have a little kid," Peichi pointed out. "Imagine a little child all excited to dig into some macaroni and cheese and then he or she comes across a chunk of sausage. Gross! I *hated* sausage when I was little."

"Okay! Okay! Forget the sausage," Natasha gave in. "Plain old mac and cheese will be fine."

Molly's pizza cheese stretched out from her mouth, refusing to separate from the pizza slice. Giggling, she put the slice of pizza down and chewed the bite in her mouth. "Okay!" she said. "You guys can come over to our house tomorrow at noon. We'll figure out what ingredients we have and then we'll figure out what we have to shop for from there and after we—"

The girls followed Molly's stunned gaze as she stared at the front door. Shawn had just walked in. Several other cheerleaders were with her, including Angie Martinez, the most stuck-up girl in all of Windsor Middle School.

"I thought Shawn couldn't come out," Amanda said, sounding both shocked and angry.

Shawn had been laughing, but her smile faded when she noticed her friends staring at her. She wiggled her fingers at them in a guilty, self-conscious greeting.

The Chef Girls waved in return, but their expressions remained unsmiling.

Angie also saw the girls staring. She flipped her hair in their direction and turned her back.

"I can't believe it!" Molly said quietly. "Would she really ditch us just to hang out with them?"

"Why don't you ask her? Here she comes," Amanda said sharply.

"Hi," Shawn said when she arrived at their table.

"I thought you had to stay home tonight." Molly got to the point right away.

Shawn laughed nervously. She removed her glasses and wiped them on her shirt. "Oh, yeah, well, after the game Dad changed his mind and said I could go out," she said, continuing to clean her glasses. "I tried to find you, but you guys had already left, and I didn't know where you were going tonight."

The girls nodded. Molly thought that Shawn could be telling the truth. She was their friend and they didn't think she would lie to them. But Amanda wasn't so sure.

"Shawn," Peichi said to her, "we're getting together tomorrow to cook for my new neighbors at Molly and Amanda's. Can you come?"

Angie arrived at their table. "Did I hear right? Are you girls playing in the kitchen again tomorrow? It's *so* cute—really adorable. Personally, I stopped playing house in the third grade, but everyone's different. Some people grow up sooner than others."

The girls tried to ignore her. "So? Can you come?" Peichi asked again.

"Yeah, I think so. Okay," Shawn agreed.

"Oh, look!" Angie said, her eyes sparkling with sudden interest. "There's Justin. Let's go say hi to him."

She turned sharply and hurried toward the table where Justin, Connor, and Omar sat. They poked intently at Gameboys while somehow managing to eat pizza at the same time.

Shawn glanced at their table and then back at her friends. "Okay, see you guys tomorrow," she said. Her parting smile was quick and unhappy as she left to follow Angie.

Amanda sat back in her chair, stunned. Was Angie going after Justin now? Why didn't Shawn stop her? Shawn *knew* that Amanda had a crush on Justin. How could she just follow Angie over there?

"Did you see that?" Amanda cried. "Shawn just ditched us! She definitely ditched us!"

Everyone looked uncomfortable.

"Manda, it's okay," Molly said quietly. "Shawn will come over tomorrow to cook. She's not ditching us—she's just hanging out with other friends sometimes."

There was a long silence. Then Natasha looked at her watch and cleared her throat. "Um, my parents will be picking me up really soon," she said. "I'm going to stand by the window to watch for them. See you guys tomorrow! Call me if you want me to bring anything." As Natasha left, she gently patted Amanda's shoulder.

Amanda smiled a little, but she still looked upset. She couldn't take her eyes off Angie, who looked like she was seriously flirting with Justin.

"Molly?" Amanda asked. "Do you mind if I call Mom for a ride home?" Molly nodded in agreement.

For Amanda, at least, the fun night was over.

## chapter 2

"Natasha, Hanukkah is a *family* holiday," Mrs. Ross said firmly. "It's not a time for friends."

"But my friends *are* like family. Don't you always tell me that family is made up of the special people you love, and not just the people you're related to? Don't you *always* say that?" Natasha insisted. "Besides, there are eight nights of the holiday. I only want to invite them for *one* of the nights."

"I don't know," Mrs. Ross said doubtfully.

"Don't you want me to be proud of our Jewish traditions?" Natasha pressed.

Mrs. Ross sighed.

Natasha took this as a sign that she was weakening. "Please, please, please," Natasha pleaded. "I think they would really like to come over. *I'd* really like to have them over. I *promise* I'll help with dinner and I'll clean up the kitchen afterward, too!"

"Remember, Natasha, we agreed you'd do some chores around here on Saturdays!" Mrs. Ross said. "You haven't done *one* thing I've asked you to do. I want you to start with your bedroom *right now*."

"I will," Natasha said, "but I already told my friends I

would help cook some food for Peichi's new neighbors. I was supposed to be there at noon and it's already twelve-fifteen."

Mrs. Ross frowned at Natasha. "When do you plan to return?"

"Before four. Definitely by four-thirty." Natasha headed for the front hall closet and pulled out her heaviest winter jacket, the puffy blue one. "No later than four-forty-five at the most," she promised.

"I expect to see you here by four-thirty and not a minute after," Mrs. Ross called as Natasha went out her front door. Natasha didn't answer, pretending she hadn't heard.

A blast of cold air hit her face. Little pockets of shiny, slippery ice glistened on the front steps. On the street, people walked with their heads down against the wind, their scarves flapping behind them.

Natasha tucked her head into her jacket. She flipped up her hood and snapped the top snaps. Luckily, she always left a pair of stretchy black gloves in her pocket. She pulled them on as quickly as possible and headed to the Moore's house.

"*Ohmygosh*, your nose is bright red," Amanda giggled as she opened the door for Natasha.

Natasha stepped into the Moore's front hall. "*Mmmm.* I smell tomato sauce cooking."

"It's for the lasagna," Amanda said. "It's so cold today that none of us wanted to go out and buy a chicken. We already had the ingredients for the lasagna right here in the refrigerator downstairs."

Shawn's Grandma Ruthie had lent the girls some money for a small fridge to hold their supplies. They kept it in the Moores' basement. The girls were able to pay Grandma Ruthie back with the money they earned on their first job. Soon Dish was doing so well that the girls chose Peichi to be the treasurer. Each week, the girls chipped in some of the money they earned for food and other supplies they'd need for their cooking jobs.

Natasha shrugged out of her jacket and hung it in the front hall closet. "That was a good idea. I'm really glad we don't have to go to the store! I sure don't want to go back out there into the cold."

She followed Amanda down the hall to the kitchen. The Chef Girls almost always cooked in the Moores' large kitchen. It was a great room to hang out in, with pale yellow walls and bright tiles. Big windows let in sunshine from the garden outside. Copper pans hung on racks and there was a huge kitchen table. The Moores' kitchen was the kind of room that welcomed everyone who entered.

The smell of seasoned tomatoes and the sound of

laughing voices grew stronger as Amanda and Natasha neared the kitchen.

"Just in time!" Shawn greeted her. "You can help me take these lasagna noodles out of this pot."

"You'd better help her quickly," Molly said with a smile. She stood at the counter tearing up lettuce leaves and tossing them into a salad spinner. "The noodles keep wrapping around her. She's going to turn into a lasagna noodle mummy if she's not careful."

Shawn laughed. "It's true. They're sticking to me and they're really hot! Ouch!"

Shawn was her old fun self. All the uneasiness from the night before seemed to have been forgotten. All the girls were together again—as they hadn't been in a while. Once more they were the Chef Girls, laughing and having a blast cooking.

"I told you to put oil in the water," Peichi said from the kitchen table where she was grating mozzarella cheese.

"I know, I know," Shawn replied. "But I forgot—and now I'm paying the price!"

"When we make lasagna again, we should try those no-cook noodles, the kind that get soft in the oven," Amanda suggested. She started chopping vegetables for the lasagna.

"That sounds good," Shawn agreed.

Natasha took a wooden spoon from the utensil drawer

and began helping Shawn lift the noodles from the large pot of hot water. Together they laid them flat on sheets of foil laid out on the kitchen table.

As the girls were working, Mrs. Moore walked into the kitchen. "It's like a sauna in here," she said with a laugh.

"Sorry, Mom," Amanda said. "We needed to boil a pot of water for the lasagna noodles. And we started another one for the macaroni we're going to cook."

"That's okay," Mrs. Moore said. She brushed her dark hair away from her face and looked around at the busy girls. "Do you think you could make some extra of something for dinner tonight?" she asked.

"We'll make some extra mac and cheese," Molly agreed.

"Okay," Mom said. "I'll fry up some sausage to put in it."

"See!" Natasha cried. "They *do* go together." She turned to Mrs. Moore. "Did you see that recipe in a magazine?"

"Yes, I did. It reminded me of when I was a child and my mother used to put chopped up hot dogs in her macaroni-and-cheese casserole."

"*Ewwwwwwww!*" the girls groaned in one voice. Even Natasha looked grossed out.

"It was good," Mrs. Moore insisted with a smile. "Really."

"Mom, please don't do it," Molly pleaded. "Or at least don't make us eat it."

"All right. I'll keep the sausage on the side," she agreed.

"Thank you," Amanda said, sounding relieved.

"You're welcome." Mrs. Moore left the kitchen, shaking her head and chuckling.

"Your mom's cool," Shawn said with a hint of sadness in her voice. Her own mother had died several years ago, after a long illness. Now she lived with her dad, whom she adored. But she still really missed her mother a lot. The twins were like Shawn's second family, but no one could replace her mom.

"Thanks," Amanda and Molly said together, their voices overlapping.

Talking about mothers reminded Natasha of the argument she'd had with her mother that morning. She was sure no one would ever call *her* mother cool. In fact, she suspected that her friends didn't like her mother very much. Her mother made them nervous because she was so strict and, well, stiff.

"Okay, we can start building this lasagna now," Shawn announced. The girls had made lasagna before, but they still needed the help of a cookbook.

Molly held the cookbook up for all to see. "Look at this book!" she said, laughing. "What a mess!" The cookbook was smeared with dried tomato sauce left over from the last time they cooked.

"I guess we're not the neatest chefs in the world," Amanda said. She put the large pan down on the table.

Molly spread some sauce on the bottom of the pan.

"Here goes," Shawn said, carefully lifting a noodle. Before she could lay it down, it had somehow folded in half and stuck together. "Argh!" she shouted in frustration.

"Just hold still," Natasha advised. Carefully, she peeled down the bottom half of the stuck noodle. Together they placed it over the sauce. Working together, they placed down an entire layer of noodles.

Molly covered the noodles with more sauce. Then Amanda put down a layer of chopped vegetables. Peichi sprinkled in the grated mozzarella. "Here we go again," Shawn said when it was time to put in a second layer of noodles. This time, though, she and Natasha got the hang of it and the whole process was easier. In about another ten minutes, they had finished assembling the lasagna. Molly sprinkled Parmesan cheese on the final layer.

"I'm not picking up the pan," Amanda said. "What if I drop it? You'll all hate me forever."

"Not *forever*," Peichi teased.

"*I'll* carry it to the oven," Molly said. She lifted the heavy pan and the top layer began to slide. "Maybe *not*," she said, putting it down quickly.

"We can do it together," Shawn suggested.

Amanda opened the oven door. The others each held the pan on one side and managed to get it inside the

17

oven. "Do you think we made too much?" Molly asked.

"Definitely," Amanda said.

"They can freeze it and have it another night," Peichi suggested.

"Yeah, like *many* other nights," Shawn said with a little laugh.

While the lasagna cooked, the girls prepared their macaroni and cheese. They cooked it in the oven along with the lasagna. Molly finished the salad she'd begun.

Peichi and Natasha made garlic bread. Amanda and Shawn whipped up a batch of brownies for dessert.

Mr. Moore came into the kitchen. "I don't have to worry about heating this house with you girls around," he said. "It's hot in here. So, when do we eat?"

"Sorry, Dad," Amanda said. "This food isn't for us. We're taking it to Peichi's new neighbors."

"Oh, that's no fair," he complained, but his blue eyes were twinkling from behind his glasses.

"We did promise Mom some extra mac and cheese for dinner tonight," Molly offered.

"Hmmm, I seem to remember we just had mac and cheese a few days ago," Mr. Moore said.

"I think we could cut off some lasagna," Peichi suggested. "We have a ton of it!"

"I've always liked you, Peichi," Mr. Moore said, patting her shoulder.

Just then, Matthew, the twins' seven-year-old brother, came into the kitchen. He held his arms stretched in front as if he were a sleepwalker or hypnotized. "Brownies," he chanted. "Smell brownies. Must have brownies. Need brownies."

"Okay, Matthew, I guess we can spare one or two," Shawn told him. "But not until they've cooled off a little!"

Matthew snapped out of his trance. "All right!" he cheered, giving a thumbs-up.

"This family is so greedy!" Amanda said, sighing.

"Sorry, hon," her father said. "It all just smells so good."

By three o'clock the girls had all the food packed in cardboard boxes. They made sure to tape their business cards to a few of the plastic containers, then bundled up and headed toward Peichi's house.

"There's the moving truck!" Molly said. Her breath made little puffs of steam in the frosty air. A huge truck sat double-parked in the street. Cars slowed to get around it. Two men struggled to carry a large, green velvet sofa up the front steps.

The girls followed the moving men up the stairs. The door at the top was held open by a piece of wood wedged under the bottom. "Hello?" they called into the hall as the men turned left with the couch.

A pretty blonde woman came down the hallway stairs. She held an adorable Asian baby in her arms. "Hi. Can I help you?"

"Hel-*lo!* I'm Peichi Cheng," cried Peichi. "I'm your new neighbor on the right side. These are my friends. We made some food to welcome you to the neighborhood."

"How lovely of you!" the woman said. "Please, come in. Let's go to the kitchen." They followed her down the hall to the kitchen in the back of the house. "Warren," she called. "We have company!"

A man stepped out of the hallway bathroom. He seemed to be in his late twenties, about the same age as his wife. "Hi, girls," he said, looking just a bit baffled to see them.

The movers hadn't unloaded the kitchen table, so the girls laid the boxes on the kitchen counters. "I'm Leslie Mink, and this is my husband, Warren," the woman said. "This is our daughter, Joli. She's one and just woke up from her nap."

Joli giggled and bounced in her mother's arms.

"She's really cute," Peichi said. "Can I hold her?"

"Sure," Mrs. Mink agreed as she handed Joli to Peichi.

"Where do you want the rest of this stuff?" one of the moving men called from down the hall.

"Could you girls watch Joli for one moment while

Warren and I go talk to the moving men?" Mrs. Mink asked.

"Okay," Peichi said. "We'll take good care of her." She sat on the floor with Joli in her lap.

"She could be your little sister," Molly said.

"I know," Peichi agreed. "She's so cute."

"And you're so modest," Shawn teased with a smile.

"Oh, you know what I mean," Peichi said. "We're both Chinese—*and* cute!"

Joli frowned. She turned her head to look for her mother. Her lower lip quivered. It looked like she was going to cry. "Why don't you read her a book?" Molly suggested. "It might distract her."

Amanda went into the living room and brought back a stack of picture books she'd found in an open box of toys. The one on top was called *The Day We Met You.* "This one looks cute," she said, handing it to Peichi.

Mrs. Mink returned and Joli stretched her arms up for her mother. "She missed you. I was about to read her this book," Peichi said.

"She loves that one," Mrs. Mink said. "It's about adoption. She doesn't understand it yet, of course. But someday, I hope, she'll understand how much we love her. We had to travel all the way to China just to adopt her."

"I'd love to go to China someday," Peichi said. "My grandparents were born there."

21

"What a gorgeous country," Mrs. Mink told Peichi. "We didn't see as much of it as I would have liked because we were so busy with paperwork, and we wanted to spend every minute with Joli. The whole process wasn't easy, but now we're so happy to have her. I can't imagine life without her!"

Natasha caught her breath, and everyone turned around to look at her. Her face was pinched in an unhappy expression. Tears rolled down her cheeks.

"What's wrong?" Molly asked.

Natasha opened her mouth to speak, but then shook her head and dashed out of the kitchen.

"**N**atasha! Wait!" Molly called. As the others stared, Molly ran out the front door and followed Natasha down the street. Natasha finally stopped running but she didn't turn around. When Molly reached her, she was out of breath. "What's wrong?" she panted.

"I don't want to talk about it," Natasha said, wiping tears from her eyes.

"Why not?" Molly pressed. "What happened? What's going on?"

Natasha just walked away quickly. Molly ran alongside her. "You're freaking me out, Natasha. Why can't you even talk about it?"

Natasha stopped and spoke through her tears. "I really, *really* don't want to talk about it. Please, just leave me alone. I have to go home!"

Molly stood and watched as Natasha walked away with her head down and her hands shoved deeply into her jacket pockets.

She turned back toward the Minks' house. The door was still open, so she walked right in and down to the kitchen. "Is your friend all right?" Mrs. Mink asked.

"What's the matter with Natasha?" asked Peichi, who was still holding Joli.

"She wouldn't tell me," Molly reported.

"Could she be having problems at home?" suggested Mrs. Mink.

Molly shrugged. "She never said anything was wrong. Although earlier she told me that she had a fight with her mother this morning."

"That's true," Amanda remembered. "But why would some baby books make her cry?"

"Natasha can be very...well..." Peichi started to tell Mrs. Mink.

"But she's changed a lot," Amanda interrupted. "She's much better than she used to be."

"That's for sure," Shawn agreed. There was a time when they'd really despised Natasha. Last year, she'd spread a lie about Molly and Amanda, and told the entire school that the twins had cheated on an important test. Then when Shawn defended the girls, Natasha lied again, saying that Shawn had cheated, too. When Natasha showed up in the girls' summer cooking class, things were really unpleasant at first. But Natasha slowly became nicer—probably because the twins, at Mrs. Moore's request, went out of their way to be nice to her. It hadn't been easy for the twins, but their patience had paid off.

Mrs. Mink smiled gently. "Well, I hope she feels happier soon. Everyone has bad days. In fact, I was having one until you girls came along. Moving is *so* stressful. Now, though, I feel so welcome here. Thank you so much for the food." She peeked into one of the boxes. "Wow! This looks fantastic. I can't wait to eat! You girls really did a lot. Thanks again."

Peichi handed Joli back to Mrs. Mink. "If you need anything, my family and I are right next door. And if you ever need a baby-sitter, I'd *love* to take care of her. She's so cute."

"You'll be seeing a lot of us," Mrs. Mink said as she walked the girls to the front door. She kicked the wooden wedge out from under the door. "I don't care what those moving men want. I can't keep this door open another second. It's freezing!"

Shawn sighed and held up the remote control. *Click!* "The band that changed grunge rock forever—their very private story!" the announcer said.

*A bunch of old guys,* she thought. *Who cares?*
*Click!*

"The Rolling Stones Story!" said the announcer on the next channel.

*Even older guys!* Shawn thought in frustration. *Where are all the cool videos?* The only good thing about her father going out on a date was that she got to watch rock videos. Her father didn't approve of them. Shawn's dad was a professor at Brooklyn College, and his idea of great TV was watching the news.

She flipped through ten more channels before giving up. "How could there be *nothing* on TV?" she said, clicking the set off.

The apartment suddenly seemed very quiet—and very empty. She glanced at some magazines on the table. No, if she read them, the house would still be too quiet. There was some homework to do. No, same problem—too quiet. *Besides,* Shawn thought, *who wants to do homework on a Saturday night? It's bad enough that I'm stuck at home!*

She stood and stretched out her arms. "Who's the team that's so cool!" she practiced the new cheer the team had just learned. "Windsor Warriors really rule!" She wasn't quite sure when she should lift her arms. Then, Shawn knew just what to do.

She'd call Angie! Angie was really fun.

Molly and Amanda were out to dinner with their family. Peichi wasn't around because her family was celebrating her grandfather's birthday. And Natasha—well, who knew what was going on with her? She probably wasn't in the mood to talk—not after the scene she had caused that afternoon.

But Angie also had a single parent—her mother. She'd mentioned to Shawn that her mother also had a date tonight.

Shawn grabbed the cordless phone, threw herself onto the couch, and punched in Angie's number. "A little too quiet for you?" she asked when Angie answered.

Angie could tell Shawn's voice right away. "Totally," she agreed. "I could be out doing something, but my mother says she doesn't want me out when she's out. Is that lame or what?"

Angie's words made Shawn crack up. "My father says the *exact same thing.* Exact! Why do I have to be here alone just because he's out? It makes no sense."

"None," Angie agreed.

"Listen, I was practicing that cheer we learned yesterday. Should I lift my arms on the 'cool,' or wait until we say 'Windsor Warriors'?"

Angie hummed through the cheer, to remind herself how it went. "Windsor Warriors," she said.

"Then what comes next?" Shawn asked. "For some reason that cheer always mixes me up."

"Get up and I'll talk you through it."

"But I have to hold the phone," Shawn reminded her.

"Does your dad have a cell phone—one with a head-set for driving?" Angie asked.

"Great idea!" Shawn said. "I'll call you right back." Her father had walked to the restaurant to meet his date, so his phone and headset were still on the front hall table. Shawn found it and put it on. Then she called Angie back. "Okay. I'm ready." She began to cheer. "Who's the team that's really cool?"

"Arms up now," Angie instructed.

Shawn's arms shot straight up over her head. "Windsor Warriors really rule!"

This was fun. It was like having Angie right there with her.

Meanwhile, Natasha sat on her bed, her journal propped against her bent knees. *I acted*  *like such a jerk today,* she wrote. *Peichi's new neighbors must think I'm a total nutcase. I was rude to Molly, too. She was only trying to be nice. But how can I ever explain to my friends what's really bothering me? It's something I just don't want them to know about.*

She wrote another paragraph before a light knock on her door made her look up. Her mother stood in the doorway and Natasha quickly shut the journal. "May I come in?" her mother asked.

"Sure," Natasha replied.

Mrs. Ross sat on the edge of Natasha's bed. "I want to talk to you about this morning," she began. "It's been bothering me all day. I feel that I didn't behave very well. You asked me a simple question about inviting your friends over to the house and I turned it into an argument about doing chores. I don't like it when we fight."

"Me neither," Natasha said. "I should help more," she admitted. "I'll start cleaning my room tonight."

Her mother smiled and stroked Natasha's blond hair. "Thank you, sweetheart. I appreciate that. And you can have your friends over for the first night of Hanukkah. When you first suggested the idea, all I could think of was that I'd have to clean even more if we were having company. Now that your dad is out of work, I have to do all the cleaning myself. We can't afford a cleaning lady anymore." Mrs. Ross sighed. "But it's not like you invited the president or somebody," she continued.

"Mom, the house always looks fine," Natasha said. She wanted to roll her eyes, but looked at the wall instead. *Mom is* such *a perfectionist*, she thought.

"Maybe I'm too fussy," Mrs. Ross said, standing. Her eyes darted to the journal lying on the bed. "Is everything all right? Is there anything you'd like to talk about?"

"No. I feel better now. Thanks, Mom," Natasha said with a smile. Her mother stood up.

"Why don't you come downstairs, Natasha? Daddy rented a movie."

"I will in a minute, Mom. I just need to finish one thing."

Mrs. Ross smiled and left the room, softly closing the

door behind her. Natasha closed her journal and stuffed it under her mattress. She always kept it in a very special place, where it couldn't be found easily. No matter what, she didn't want anyone to read it.

Ever.

Usually Shawn found it hard to pay attention during her first Monday morning class. She wasn't quite into the swing of the school week yet. But today she sat forward in her desk, interested in what her science teacher was telling the class.

"The sixth-grade science fair is an exciting event. Every year, our sixth-grade students just amaze us with the creative, educational projects they design. You can work in a group of two to six other sixth-graders. The group members can be from any science class, as long as they are in the sixth grade. Before you decide who you'll work with, make sure you find other students with similar science interests. Don't just work with your buddies. I hope you'll all do well in this year's science fair."

Angie turned in her seat and smiled at Shawn. She pointed between herself and Shawn. She obviously wanted them to be partners.

*Uh-oh*, Shawn thought. *Not this again.* Ever since she'd become a cheerleader, she felt torn between her new cheerleading friends and her oldest and best friends, Molly and Amanda.

35

After class Angie hurried to Shawn's side. "Do you have any ideas?" she asked.

Shawn shook her head.

"Well, we'll work with some of the other girls on the team. One of them is bound to have an idea."

"Ummm..." Shawn began. "I'll probably be working with Amanda and Molly."

Angie folded her arms, swung out her right hip, stepped back, and sneered. "Are we talking about Molly *Einstein* here?"

"No. Molly Moore," Shawn replied, a little confused.

"I know! I know!" Angie said, flinging one arm into the air. "What I mean is that she's the same Molly Moore who was practically *failing* out of sixth grade until she started getting *tutored*, like, every day! Do you *really* think that's a good person to work with, Shawn?"

Shawn frowned. "She wasn't *failing*, Angie. Molly's really smart. And her grades are good now."

"Whatever," Angie sneered, rolling her eyes. She put her arm around Shawn. "Believe me," she continued, "you want to do your project with *us*—not those losers."

"They're not losers," Shawn argued. *And your grades aren't so good*, Shawn wanted to say, but didn't.

"It'll be good for the team if we all work together," Angie said, ignoring Shawn's objections. "Come on. Let's get some lunch."

Shawn stuck her head out of the classroom to make sure Molly, Amanda, Natasha, and Peichi weren't in the hall. She didn't see them. "Okay," she told Angie with a sigh. "Let's go." For some reason, Shawn felt like she had been really disloyal to the Chef Girls. *I stuck up for Molly,* she thought. *I'm allowed to work in a different group if I want to. I don't have to do* everything *with them.* In her heart, Shawn knew she would rather be working with Molly and Amanda. But something in Angie's voice made Shawn feel like she did *not* want to get on her bad side.

Molly, Amanda, and Peichi walked home together from school that afternoon. Peichi dragged her heavy backpack along the waist-high stone wall that surrounded Prospect Park. "Hey, isn't that Shawn up ahead?"

It was, so the girls ran to catch up. "Why didn't you wait for us after school?" Molly panted when they reached her.

Shawn shrugged. "I didn't see you."

"We were right in front!" Amanda said. "Can you come over? We have to start planning our science project."

"What project?" Shawn asked, feeling sick inside. She knew *exactly* what project.

"Duh! The one for the sixth-grade science fair!" Peichi said with a laugh.

"Oh, *that* project," Shawn said, feeling even sicker. She took a deep breath and then said, "I think I'll probably be working on that with Angie and some of the other girls from the team." For a moment, there was a stunned silence.

"You're not working with *us?*" Molly cried in disbelief.

"You guys should have asked me," Shawn defended herself. "I would have been in your group, but Angie asked me first."

"Oh, come on!" Amanda said. "You're our best friend. Why should we *have* to ask you? We just assumed you'd be with us."

"Well I didn't know that!" Shawn insisted. "I'm sorry, but it's just a science project. Angie asked me first. It would have been really mean for me to say 'Sorry, Angie, but I don't want to work with you.'"

"I guess," Peichi gave in with a small frown.

The four of them walked the rest of the way home together. They didn't talk and joke the way they usually did, though. Peichi, Amanda, and Molly all felt the same thing—like Shawn was very far away.

Shawn turned down her block. "Bye," she said with a wave.

"Bye," the girls replied in dull voices.

When they approached Peichi's house, she invited them to come inside.

"Thanks, but I've got too much homework," Molly declined. "I can't hang out today."

"Same here," Amanda said. "Let's just start on our science project tomorrow." Amanda didn't even feel like thinking about it anymore.

"Too bad," Peichi said. "Mrs. Mink's leaving Joli at our house for a few hours. She's so much fun to play with."

The girls left Peichi at her house and continued on toward home. "Look who's walking toward us," Amanda said. "It's Ms. Barlow."

Brenda Barlow ran the theater department at Windsor Middle School. She was *very* theatrical. Amanda had performed a small role in the fall musical, *My Fair Lady*. But the twins had first met Ms. Barlow the previous summer, when they did the cooking for a birthday party she had for her daughter. The only problem was that she forgot to pay them for almost a week!

"Amanda, darling, how *nice* to run into you! And hello, Mary dear, how are *you?*"

"Hi, Ms. Barlow," the girls greeted her. Then Molly said, "Um, it's *Molly*."

"Right you are!" declared Mrs. Barlow. "Amanda, I've been hoping to speak to you. But I just *never* see you since the play ended!"

35

"Oh?" Amanda asked.

"I was wondering if you're planning to try out for the spring play."

Amanda thought acting was the coolest thing in the world. After performing in *My Fair Lady*, she felt like she had been born to act. "I think I will, yes," she answered.

"Oh, you *absolutely* must!" Ms. Barlow cried. "You were *outstanding* in the last play and I would simply *love* to work with you again!"

A smile crossed Amanda's face. She'd never realized Ms. Barlow thought she was such a good actress.

"By the way," added Ms. Barlow, "I *also* want to talk to you girls about your little catering business."

Amanda and Molly looked at each other. They weren't exactly sure what Ms. Barlow meant by *catering*. "It's actually a cooking business," Molly explained.

"But catering is a big part of it," Amanda jumped in. It seemed very important not to disappoint or disagree with Ms. Barlow, especially when she was thinking of casting Amanda in the spring play. "We enjoy catering. And we're always looking for more catering jobs."

"Fabulous," Ms. Barlow said, clapping her hands in delight. "I'd *love* to hire you girls to cater a little holiday party I'm having! The date is Saturday, December sixteenth. Can you do it?" Ms. Barlow asked.

"Absolutely," Amanda agreed. "We'd love to."

"*Wonderful,*" Ms. Barlow said. "I'll be in touch about the details. Bye-bye."

"Bye." Amanda waved as Ms. Barlow walked off down the block.

"Amanda!" Molly scolded. "Why did you agree to cater her party?"

"She wants to put me in the spring play!"

"Don't you remember how much trouble we had getting paid the last time we made food for her?"

Amanda shrugged. "It wasn't *that* bad, Molls. She just forgot. And she did pay us eventually, remember? Plus, we did the baking for the fall play and we got paid for that."

"Fine, but we still don't even know what catering is!" Molly argued.

Amanda grinned. "Well, we'll just have to find out."

olly stretched out on her bed. She held up a thick gift catalog so that Amanda could see it from her bed. "Do you think Matthew would like this lightsaber thingy?"

Amanda glanced up from the issue of a glossy teen magazine she'd been reading. "It's totally him," she said.

"Good," Molly said, making a check mark next to the item. "That's what he's getting for Christmas from me. I'm picking all my Christmas gifts from catalogs and then ordering them off the Internet this year."

"How will you do that without a credit card?" Amanda questioned.

"Oh, I already figured that out. Mom said that if I give her my money she'll let me use her card," Molly explained. "I'm sure she'll do it for you, too."

Amanda sat up and sighed. "I have no idea what I'm getting anyone. I've been so busy—there's school and Dish and now the science fair and *everything*. I haven't even thought about Christmas presents."

"You'd better start thinking. Christmas will be here before you know it," Molly reminded her.

"What do *you* want for Christmas?" Amanda asked.

Molly thumbed through her catalog. "I want this electric grill. Wouldn't that be cool to have? We could add grilled vegetables to our menu and do lots of stuff with it. It would be great to have this deluxe food processor, too. Mom's food processor is so old, the lid doesn't even fit right!"

"How about a small wooden cutting board?" Amanda suggested. "That's about all I'd be able to afford this year—if I'm lucky."

"What do you want for Christmas?" Molly asked.

"Money!"

"No, really. What?"

Amanda thumbed through her magazine until she found the page she was searching for. "This!" she said, holding up a picture of a rock star looking awesome in a sparkly halter-top and a flowing skirt.

Molly chuckled. "Good luck! Do you know how much that probably costs?"

"Not that *exact* outfit, but something like it," Amanda said. "I also saw a madeleine pan at Park Terrace Cookware. I would *love* to have one of those!"

"A madeleine pan?" Molly asked.

"You know, those cookies that look like shells? They're really buttery and have powdered sugar

39

on them. They're called madeleines. *Mmmm,* if I had a madeleine pan I could make some of them right now!"

"Chill out, Manda! It's almost dinner time," Molly said with a laugh. Amanda *adored* sweets. "What are you getting for Mom?"

Amanda flopped down on her bed. "I have no idea! Where will I ever get the money for all these presents, anyway? How come you have so much money?"

"Well, for starters, I don't have your massive collection of clothes, hair things, and nail polish," Molly pointed out.

Amanda sighed deeply. "Oh, I'm no good at saving money. I know that. We'd better sell a lot of meals between now and then."

"We have that catering job for Ms. Barlow," Molly said hopefully.

Amanda sat up again, smiling. "That's right. I bet catering pays well—whatever it is."

"We'd better find out," Molly said, swinging her legs to the floor. "Let's go look it up on the Internet."

They hurried downstairs and found Matthew playing a computer game starring Japanese anime characters. "We need the computer," Molly told him.

"No fair!" Matthew complained.

"Yes, it is. You've been playing since you got home from school. And your eyes are all glazed over. Come on, get off," Amanda insisted. "Don't you have to practice the violin or something?"

"Well, yeah," admitted Matthew.

Still grumbling about unfairness, Matthew shut down his game and left.

"Let's check our e-mail before we look up catering," Amanda said. She quickly clicked the mail icon and, sure enough, there was an e-mail waiting for the twins.

"It's from Carmen," Amanda said happily. Carmen Piccolo had been the twins' cooking teacher. Along with her assistant, Freddie Gonzalez, she had taught a cooking class last summer in the back room of Park Terrace Cookware. Carmen and Freddie were really fun and nice, and the girls had missed them since class had ended. Amanda opened the message.

**To:** mooretimes2, happyface, qtpie490, cookincon11,
BrooklyNatasha, funnyomy478, wannabe, FredGonz528,
HomieTDog
**From:** pots-n-pans55
**Date:** 12/4, 3:22 PM
**Re:** Tis the Season for Gingerbread Houses!

Hi to all you fabulous young chefs!
    Freddie and I will be offering
a class in the fine art of making
gingerbread houses. Bring an apron
and your wonderful self to the usual
spot on Sunday, December 17, at

41

10:00 A.M. The class will probably last until 4:00 P.M.

Come for some holiday fun! I hope to see you all soon.

Carmen

"Awesome!" Amanda cried. "That's going to be so cool!"

Peichi's screen name appeared on their Buddy List. An IM box popped up on the screen almost instantly.

**happyface:** Hello! Did you see the e-mail from Carmen?

**mooretimes2:** yup! Sounds 2 kewl. ☺ R u going?

**happyface:** but of course! R u?

**mooretimes2:** Def! Wonder if Shawn will go...

**happyface:** Too busy w/cheerleaders? ☹

**mooretimes2:** Hope not. Talk to NR today?

**happyface:** a little. She seemed happier. ☺

**mooretimes2:** did she say what was wrong?

**happyface:** ☹...no...☹ I wonder what the problem is...

The computer voice told them that they had a new e-mail. Amanda clicked on the little mailbox symbol in the corner.

**To:** justmac, op87, octoberfaerie, g2mhi, snew67, sk8trboy, Mooretimes2, happyface, qtpie490, BrooklynNatasha, tygrgal, tealsky89, artsiegurl1209, angelbaby00, raptor25, Noonehere289, smileychick97, TheWilliamsFam

**From:** Cookincon11

**Date:** 12/4, 5:57 PM

**Re:** Holiday fun!

---

Hey Everyone! Connor here. My family and I are having a tree-trimming and ice-skating party. We hope this'll become an annual thing. Here's some info:

**DATE:** 12/16

**PLACE:** My house! You all know where that is. (Call for directions if you need them.)

**TIME:** from about 5:00 p.m. to around 11:00 p.m. We'll go ice skating first, then come back to my house for decorating the tree and eating lots of food!!!

**BRING:** Ice skates, warm clothes, presents for me (no way, I'm just

43

kiddin, you don't have to bring
me presents)

We will have all the food and
decorations and stuff like that...
Music too! It's gonna be SWEET. Well,
call me if you have any questions!
Hope to see you there!     —Connor

"Oooooh" Amanda squealed. "This'll be so fun! And...oh my gosh! *He'll* be there!"

Molly looked at her sister and said slowly "I'm guessing that 'he' is...Justin?"

"Who else?" Amanda sighed and dramatically put a hand over her heart. "Look—his screen name is on the invite list."

"Uh, Manda, look at the date. Saturday night... December sixteenth?"

Amanda was too busy to hear Molly. She was imagining herself skating by Justin, wearing a cute little skating skirt, doing a pretty twirl and impressing him...

"Amanda? Hello?" Molly continued. "Connor's party is on the same night as Ms. Barlow's."

"Huh? Oh, right," Amanda finally said. "I'm not worried. We can just drop off the food at Ms. Barlow's and then head straight over to Connor's house for the party. Or meet them at the skating rink if we're a little late."

The IM bell rang. Molly tapped the screen. "Peichi! We forgot about her!" "Oops!" Amanda said with a laugh. Amanda clicked over to the IM box. There were five new messages that Peichi had written while the twins where checking out the e-mail from Connor. Amanda turned to Molly and grinned sheepishly.

**happyface:** Manda? Molly?

**happyface:** hello? nobody home?

**happyface:** r u there?

**happyface:** Where did you 2 go? hello?

**happyface:** *Why did you leave me?!*

**mooretimes2:** hi, sorry. We're here.

**happyface:** I thought you two left!

**mooretimes2:** heeheehee, sorry...So, did you get the e-mail from Connor?

**happyface:** dunno...hold on, I'll check it out, brb

**mooretimes2:** k

**happyface:** back, yeah, it looks like lots of fun!

**mooretimes2:** Molly talking now, kicked Amanda off, she was hogging the computer, she had to go fix her hair or something...heeheehee...anyway, yeah, it looks like fun, but one problem...

**happyface:** ?

**mooretimes2:** We have Ms. Barlow's party to cater...

**happyface:** what? hey! no one told me about this! what's the deal?

**mooretimes2:** we ran into Ms. B after school and she asked us to cater the party. Manda and I think it will pay pretty good.

**happyface:** sweet! I will do it then.

**mooretimes2:** ummm...do you know anything about catering?

**happyface:** no, I was figuring you would...oh, please say you do!?!?

**mooretimes2:** nope...oh gosh, we're in trouble now...

**happyface:** ok, I'll try and figure out just what goes into a catering job...

**mooretimes2:** ok, thanks! We will ask mom and dad 2. Got 2 eat now. Bye.

**happyface:** byeeeeeeeee!!!!!!!! Call me later.

Molly signed off and went to the kitchen. Amanda was already there, along with her parents. They sat around the table that was already set and laid out for dinner.

"Mom, do you know anything about catering?" Molly asked as she sat.

46

"Amanda was just telling us that Dish accepted a job to cater Ms. Barlow's party," Mom said.

Dad walked over to the intercom and buzzed Matthew's room. "Come on downstairs, sport," he said. "It's time for dinner!"

"Amanda says you aren't exactly sure what catering is," their mom went on. "Girls, was it wise to accept a job when you don't know what you'll be doing?"

Amanda shrugged. "How hard could it be? We just make a lot of food, right?"

"Oh no, it's much more than that! You have to first make the food...and *lots* of it! Do you even know how many people are coming to this party? Or what kind of food Ms. Barlow wants you to prepare?"

"Well, no," Amanda admitted with a sinking feeling. "But I can call her tonight and find out."

"But preparing the food is just the beginning!" Mom continued.

"It is?" Molly asked, feeling worried.

"Absolutely. You girls will have to prepare all the food according to Ms. Barlow's menu, deliver it, arrange the food attractively on the platters, serve it, and then clean up after the party—all the dishes, everything! You'll need to stay for the entire party. And since you'll be serving, you'll all have to look nice. Ms. Barlow might even want you wearing matching outfits, like black pants and white blouses."

Together, Amanda and Molly groaned.

"Oh no...I had no idea it involved all that!" Amanda said.

Mrs. Moore smiled sympathetically. "But look on the bright side—it usually pays a lot, too!"

"Well, that doesn't hurt!" Molly said, trying to be optimistic.

"Especially not when we have so many gifts to buy," Amanda said as their mother dished out the roast beef and mashed potatoes.

"Well, we already committed to Ms. Barlow, so we're stuck doing this job even if we wanted to back out," Molly said. "Mom, can we have an emergency meeting of the Chef Girls here tomorrow?"

"I suppose so," Mrs. Moore agreed.

"Thanks!" said both twins at the same time.

Their mother laughed. "All right, but eat your dinner now, it's going to get cold."

"First I have to call Shawn to tell her!" said Molly as she rushed from the table to get the phone.

"And I should go e-mail Peichi and Natasha about the meeting!" Amanda also left the table.

"Get back here, girls!" Mrs. Moore called.

Molly and Amanda came back to the table.

"Let's eat together—as a family, please," their mom said. "You can make your calls after dinner."

After dinner was done, Amanda hopped right back on the Internet. Peichi was still online, so Amanda quickly sent her an IM.

**mooretimes2:** hi, it's Amanda, got 2 tell u something...
**happyface:** Hi, what's up?
**mooretimes2:** After school Ms. Barlow asked me and Molls to cater this party she wants to have. And we just found out that catering is a really big job. We're going to have an emergency meeting tomorrow at my place after school.
**happyface:** Ok, I'll be there. What day is Ms. Barlow's party?
**mooretimes2:** It's the 16$^{th}$
**happyface:** same day as Connor's party?

*Oh no...*Amanda thought. She needed the money from catering for Ms. Barlow. But she couldn't miss this great party and her chance to be around Justin. Peichi IM'd her again.

**happyface:** Hello? U there?
**mooretimes2:** yeah, sorry. It is the same day.
**happyface:** 2 bad

**mooretimes2:** would you email Natasha about the meeting? g2g, ttyl, bye
**happyface:** No problem! Bye again.

"So, what do you plan to do about the case of the two parties on the same day?" Molly asked as they were lying on their beds that night.

"I don't know," Amanda answered. *I'll just have to find a way to do both,* she thought to herself.

## chapter 6

"**W**hy did you take a big job like this without asking us first?" Shawn demanded. The Chef Girls were sitting in the Moore's kitchen, talking about the catering job.

"It just seemed like such a good thing. I was sure you'd all want to do it," Amanda said defensively. "Besides, couldn't *you* use the money? I know Molly and I could."

"Yeah," Shawn admitted. "The extra cash would be really helpful."

"I guess we all could," Peichi agreed.

The timer rang. Molly got oven mitts and took a tray out of the toaster oven. "Oh, they came out so cute," she said. The girls had cut pieces of white bread into circles with a cookie cutter. Then they stuffed them into the holes of a small muffin pan, forming little cups. They'd put them in the toaster oven to toast. Now they'd come out as little toast cups.

This was something Mrs. Cheng had told Peichi about after seeing them at a party she went to. "Mom said that these were filled with some creamy mushroom stuffing," Peichi had reported. "But that sounded too complicated to make for an after-school snack."

Instead, the girls came up with the idea of filling the cups with tuna salad and then sprinkling chopped cheddar cheese on top. "Like a tuna melt," Molly said. Once the cups were filled, they put them back in the oven just long enough for the cheese to melt.

"These are awesome," Shawn said when she bit into one of them.

The phone rang and Molly turned to get it, but Amanda grabbed it first. "She always does that," Molly laughed. It was true, too. Amanda had an amazing talent for *always* beating her twin to the phone.

"Oh, hi, Ms. Barlow," Amanda said. "We're all here talking about your party. Oh, okay, hang on a sec." Amanda grabbed a pen and pad from the table and returned to the phone. "I'm ready. Fifteen people. Five are vegetarians. Four of them don't eat dairy food." She paused. "Wait. Do all the vegetarians eat dairy?"

"Oh, please let them eat dairy," Shawn said. "Otherwise what will we give them—leaves?"

Peichi tapped Amanda's arm. "Ask her if the vegetarians who don't eat dairy are vegans," she said.

"Ms. Barlow, hold on," Amanda said. She covered the mouthpiece. "Peichi, what is a *vegan?*" she whispered.

"A vegan doesn't eat any animal products—not dairy, or eggs, or even honey. Just check to make sure!" Peichi replied.

"Okay, I'm back," Amanda said into the phone. "Now,

are any of the guests vegans? That's a vegetarian who doesn't eat any animal products," Amanda said, trying to sound knowledgeable. "No? Okay. Now, for the menu... A buffet? That's fine. Dessert? We were thinking festive...Christmas cookies, that sort of thing...we know how to make pie. We even learned how to make our own crust in cooking class. Oh, apple crisp? I think we can do that...Okay, thanks, Ms. Barlow. Bye."

Amanda looked down at her notes, then faced her friends. "She's not picky about the menu, as long as it is *elegant* and *delicious!*" Amanda struck a dramatic pose, imitating Ms. Barlow. "She said she wants us to have *creative freedom* with the menu. And she wants an absolutely *marvelous, fabulous* array of desserts!"

"Oh, is that all?" Shawn said. "How much is she paying us for all this?"

"We haven't really talked about money," Amanda admitted. "We'll do it next time she calls."

"We'd better," Molly agreed. "All this food is going to cost a lot, plus we're going to be doing a ton of work."

"I think I'll ask my mom to teach me how to make little cards on the computer to place by each dish on the buffet. That way, the vegetarians and the people who don't eat dairy food will know what they can eat," Peichi suggested.

"That's a really good idea!" said Natasha.

Amanda took five cookbooks down from the kitchen bookshelf. She staggered back under their weight before dropping them on the table with a loud *thunk*. "We'd better start finding recipes," she said.

"First let's talk about what we already know how to make," Natasha suggested. "A good vegetarian appetizer is hummus. That's made from chickpeas. And baba ghanouj—it's made out of roasted eggplant. We can serve both of those with warm pita bread. I *love* that."

"We could make baked brie," Amanda suggested.

"What's that?" Peichi asked.

"Brie is a kind of cheese," Amanda explained. "It has this kinda hard white stuff on the outside, called rind, and the inside is soft and yummy!"

"Sounds delicious!" Peichi said.

"To bake it, you wrap it in pastry, like Phyllo dough, and you bake it in the oven until it gets all warm and gooey," Amanda continued.

"This cookbook has the baked brie made two different ways. I'll put a bookmark in here."

Shawn thumbed through *Dish*, the cookbook that the girls were putting together. It contained all their favorite recipes. "Carmen's biscotti cookies are pretty fabulous," she said, finding the recipe in the book.

"We also have a recipe in there for pie crust," Peichi

said to Shawn. "We could make an apple pie. Or pumpkin."

The girls got to work putting together old recipes and new ones. The kitchen grew unusually quiet. Only the sound of turning pages broke the stillness.

After several minutes, Natasha spoke. "I asked Mom if I could invite you guys over for the first night of Hanukkah and she said yes. So, um, do you think you might want to come?"

"We'll have to ask," Molly answered. Mrs. Ross wasn't her favorite person. She was so formal. Molly knew Amanda felt the same way. The idea of spending an entire evening with her wasn't too appealing. But for Natasha's sake she'd be willing to do it. "I don't see why not," she added.

"Yeah, I bet Mom will say yes," Amanda agreed.

"My dad will probably say okay," Shawn said.

"My parents, too," said Peichi. "It sounds like fun. Do we have to bring gifts or food?"

"No, you don't have to worry about that. My mom will take care of everything."

"You're lucky," Peichi said. "You don't have to wait as long for your gifts, and you have eight nights of gift giving."

"That's true, but it's just one gift a night," Natasha reminded her.

"I guess so," Peichi said. "I asked for new in-line skates

and I'm going crazy wondering if I'll get them. I wish I could find out sooner."

"Natasha, is it weird for you, not celebrating Christmas?" Shawn asked. "I mean, do you feel, like, left out?"

Natasha thought about this question for a moment. "When I was little I felt that way," she admitted. "I wondered why Santa didn't give gifts to Jewish kids. It kind of hurt my feelings, you know."

"You must have thought Santa was a big creep!" Peichi exclaimed.

"Sometimes I did, but mostly I just didn't understand it," Natasha said.

"Do you still feel bad about it?" Amanda asked.

"No," Natasha said. "Not at all. I understand it now—it's just how different religions are celebrated. And it's not like I sit around on Christmas feeling sad that I don't have a bunch of presents to open. Every Christmas morning my parents and I go serve a Christmas breakfast at the homeless shelter."

"Wow!" said Shawn. "That's really nice of you."

"Majorly nice," Peichi agreed.

"It really is," Molly said. She tried to picture Mrs. Ross smiling and being jolly on Christmas. It was hard to imagine. Still, she was doing a good thing, so maybe she had a kind heart, even though she usually seemed so stern.

Natasha smiled. "It's my family's tradition. And we usually go to a movie afterward, which is fun, too."

Matthew came into the kitchen with his best friend and neighbor, Ben Bader. "Hey, I smell something good," he said. "Can we have some?"

There were four tuna cups left in the tray. "Help yourselves," Molly offered. Matthew couldn't get his cup out of the tray and wound up with a handful of warm, cheesy tuna. He flipped it into his mouth with a loud popping sound. Then he stuck the small toast cup on his nose. "Hey, I'm a pig. Oink! Oink!"

"You sure are," Amanda quipped. She took a tuna toast cup out of the tray and handed it to Ben. "Now get out of here, you two, we're trying to work."

"This is good," Ben said as he and Matthew left.

"Oink!" Matthew shouted.

"Little boys are so crazy," Peichi said, smiling.

"*All* boys are crazy," Shawn added.

Talking about boys made Amanda remember Connor's party. "I wonder how late Ms. Barlow's party will go," she said. "Connor's party ends at about eleven. Maybe we can catch the second half of it." She pictured Justin sitting there at the party, looking bored and then suddenly smiling brightly when she arrived.

"Forget it," Molly said. "The Barlow party can't possibly end before ten. By the time we clean up it will definitely be past eleven."

"We can clean up as we go," Amanda suggested.

"Maybe," Molly said. "But we'll be serving. Remember?"

Amanda sighed and sunk into her chair. This was no fair. There *had* to be a way she could do both things.

Shawn looked up at the clock and jumped up from her chair. "I didn't realize it was so late!" she cried. "I've got to go!"

"Where are you going?" Peichi asked.

"Ummm..." Shawn mumbled. "Uh...the, uh...my science group is getting together to plan our science project."

The Chef Girls exchanged quick glances. "What's your project on?" Molly asked.

"We're not sure yet," Shawn said. "Bye."

"*She* sure left fast," Amanda grumbled when Shawn was gone. "I guess she was in a hurry to get to her new friends."

"She was late," Peichi offered.

"Well, I guess we should start working on our science project, too," stated Molly.

Amanda tipped her chair back and balanced on it. "I wonder what their project will be—probably the science of cheerleading. I can just imagine it." She began speaking in a high, squeaky voice. "During this cheer we will stick our arms out at a fifty-degree angle. These cheers are very scientific."

The girls laughed at this. "No, they'll do that pyramid they do at games and call it ancient Egyptian science," Peichi said.

Amanda straightened her chair with a hard *clunk* on the floor. She sat forward and thrust her chin into her hands. "What does she see in those girls, anyway?" she asked. "Angie Martinez is *so* stuck-up. I think it's disloyal of Shawn to be friends with someone who is so rude to us. It's like she doesn't even care how mean Angie is to her best friends—like it's okay with her. Ever since she became a cheerleader, everything's changed. She's been our best friend since we were little and now cheerleading has ruined everything!"

Molly cleared her throat. "Manda, you need to chill a little about this whole thing with Shawn and the cheerleaders. Mom said we'd all be making new friends once we got to middle school—and she was right. I'm friends with Athena, you're friends with Tessa. And Shawn's friends with Angie."

Amanda said seriously, "I know, Molls. And I don't mind if Shawn has other friends, like we do. But the difference is that our friends aren't always putting Shawn down. They're nice to her, like they're nice to us. But Angie either ignores us or makes fun of us. And she does it right in front of Shawn, and Shawn doesn't say *any-thing* to her—she doesn't even tell her to cut it out. All I

59

know is that I would never let *anyone* talk about my friends the way Angie does."

There was an awkward silence. No one seemed to know what to say. Amanda was definitely mad, but she'd made a good point. Did Shawn even care how her new friends treated her old friends? And if she did care, why didn't she act like it?

For the rest of that day, and all the next, Amanda set her mind to one single problem: how she could cater Ms. Barlow's holiday affair and still make it to Connor's party.

"Manda, you're not paying attention," Molly said in frustration Wednesday night after supper. They sat together in the kitchen.

"What's that?" Amanda asked. "What did you say?"

"*Hello!* We're supposed to be deciding on the menu for the Barlow party."

"Didn't we do that already?"

"No! We had a preliminary menu. And now we need to make the final menu. Come *on*, Manda! I really need your help with all this!"

The phone rang. Amanda grabbed it. "Hi, Ms. Barlow!"

Molly rolled her eyes. "Not again," she muttered. This made the seventh call they'd received from her since they'd taken the job.

"Oh, yes, we're in excellent shape with the menu," Amanda said to her. "Here's what I think we should serve. For appetizers, we'll have baked brie two ways—one with

mustard and one with apples and honey—hummus and baba ghanouj with warm pita bread, stuffed mushrooms, warm artichoke dip, and scallops wrapped in bacon."

Molly's jaw dropped. She had no idea Amanda had even been listening to her.

"Yes, sure," she went on. "The main dishes will be roast turkey, marinated portobello mushrooms over egg fettuccine, cold wild rice salad with dried cranberries, chef salad, and green beans with toasted almonds." She grabbed Molly's notebook off the table and glanced at the page. "So that gives us seven dishes without meat, six dishes without dairy, and five dishes without meat *or* dairy." Amanda paused to take a deep breath.

"Desserts? Oh, of course. We'll have lots of different holiday cookies, minted grapefruit salad, and apple crisp. It will all be very *festive*, I promise! Thanks, Ms. Barlow. Bye." Amanda hung up the phone. "Let's hope that will be the last phone call from Ms. Barlow—for a few days, at least!"

"Wow, Manda! I guess you *were* paying attention after all," Molly said. "All that food sounds so *good*! I wish we could eat it right now."

"I have been listening to you, even though it doesn't seem that way," Amanda said. "Half of my brain has been listening, but half of it is thinking about something else."

"Connor's party, right?"

Amanda nodded.

"Forget about it," Molly said bluntly. "There's no way you can go. You're the one who told Ms. Barlow we'd do this catering thing. Remember?"

Amanda nodded. "By the way, she just told me that this party is going to be fancy, so we'll have to dress up. At least we won't have to all wear matching black and white outfits like Mom mentioned!"

"It's *fancy*? Oh, no! That's terrible!" Molly whined. "What am I going to wear?"

Amanda smiled. "We'll just have to go shopping and get some fancy clothes!" she said. This idea brightened her mood.

"Who has money to shop for new clothes at this time of year?" Molly retorted. "Come upstairs with me and look in the closet. Maybe we can dig up something from last Christmas. I can't believe this. I think this should be the last job we do for Ms. Barlow. This party is such a hassle, it makes me sick."

"Be right there," Amanda called as Molly left the kitchen. Molly's words had inspired her. Then an idea hit her.

*I got it!* she said to herself. *I'll pretend to be sick!*

The plan was so simple, yet so brilliant. She'd work the party until seven or eight o'clock. Then she'd suddenly be struck ill—maybe get a bad headache or a really sore throat. Ms. Barlow had said she was a good actress. She could probably act sick without too much trouble. Amanda had had strep throat last winter, and she still remembered how *awful* she had felt.

*This is awesome!* she thought. *Everything's gonna work out now!*

Then Amanda squirmed uneasily in her chair. She had to admit that this wasn't exactly a nice thing to do to Molly and her friends. It wasn't right to leave them behind to clean up while she went off to have fun at a party.

But she *would* make it up to them. It would be fair as long as she did more than her share in the beginning. She'd get there early and set up everything before the rest arrived. That way it would be *totally* fair if she left early. Besides, *she'd* gotten them the job in the first place, and now they were all going to make a *ton* of money. She deserved a little something extra for that!

*Absolutely,* she decided. *I'm gonna do it!*

Suddenly, Molly appeared in the kitchen door dressed in crumpled black velvet pants and a wrinkled white ruffled shirt. "How about this?"

Amanda was startled out of her thoughts. "Huh?" She

eyed Molly critically. "Molls, did you even look in the mirror?" she asked with a sigh.

"What do you mean?" Molly asked.

"Didn't you wear that outfit for the holiday chorus show last year?"

"Yeah. So?"

"Look down at your ankles."

Molly gazed down. "Okay, so the pants have gotten a little short. Mom can probably let out the hems."

"I don't think so. Those pants are *really* short, Molls," Amanda disagreed. "And that shirt looks like it's been wadded up at the bottom of your closet for nearly a year."

"Okay, well, maybe it has..." Molly admitted with a sheepish grin. "Maybe Mom can iron it. Or I can bring it to the cleaners or something."

Amanda patted her twin's shoulder. "Don't worry. We'll find you something to wear."

Molly sighed. "Fashion just isn't my thing."

"Well, I'll go find something for you. You *are* my size, after all!" Amanda said with a grin as she left the kitchen table.

Molly sat at the table and began to think about how bad Amanda must feel about missing Connor's party. *Manda's being really great about it, though,* she thought. *She's not complaining that much or pouting or anything.* Molly grabbed an apple and got up to wash it. Suddenly she had another one of her great ideas. *I know! We'll have our own party! It'll be a blast! Amanda won't mind missing Connor's party if she has another party to look forward to!*

Amanda returned to the kitchen holding her knee-length black satin skirt with the flounce at the hem, and a green-and-white flowered blouse. "Here, Molls, you can borrow my skirt. And with this green top, and maybe a green barrette and a necklace, you'll look really pretty and Christmasy. This outfit looks really good on me," she said. "And if it looks good on *me*, it'll look good on *you!*"

"I guess that's true," Molly said, with a little laugh. They *were* identical twins, after all! "But can I borrow some pants instead?"

"Molls, the skirt will look really *nice,*" Amanda persisted with a little pout.

"Fine, Manda. Hey, listen, I just had a brilliant idea! Let's have a New Year's Eve sleepover! I know you're bummed about missing Connor's party, so this'll be a good substitute!"

"That *is* a good idea!" Amanda agreed. "It'll be really fun!" She started feeling a little queasy about her plan to skip out on the end of the Barlow job. Now Molly was trying really hard to plan something special for her, and she was planning to ditch Dish in the middle of their biggest job ever.

"I knew you'd think that! I'll go ask Mom and Dad. They just *have* to say yes!" Molly said as she rushed up the stairs to her parent's bedroom.

*Yeah, it* will *be fun, but it won't be a substitute for Connor's party,* Amanda thought. She bit her lip.

Molly ran back down the stairs again. "Mom and Dad said yes!" she cried. "I know—let's go think of some good foods we can serve for a...Chef Girls'-style New Year's Day brunch!"

"Okay!" Amanda said, but her mind was still on Connor's party.

"Maybe we could find something more interesting than pulleys," Shawn suggested. She was at the school library along with Angie and three other girls from the cheerleading team—Stephanie Fisher, Jessica Silvia, and Ashley Brothers. Shawn sat at a long table in the Research section, staring at a printout of the computer search she'd just done on pulleys.

"What's wrong with pulleys?" asked Angie.

Angie didn't wait for Shawn to reply. Instead, she turned to Stephanie. "Who do you think is hotter, Justin McElroy or Chris Ratner?" she asked, comparing Justin McElroy with another boy in their grade.

"Oh, most definitely Chris," answered Stephanie.

"Are you nuts?" cried Jessica. "Justin is way hotter!"

"I think so, too," Angie said.

"Justin is your hottie now, huh?" Stephanie teased Angie.

Angie smiled slyly. "So, what if he is?"

Shawn just sighed. *Do these girls think about anything beside boys? I should so be with the Chef Girls right now! Why in the world did I tell Angie I'd work with her and the cheerleaders? This project is going to be a disaster.*

"Okay, girls, tell me this. Why on *earth* is Daria McHenry going out with Josh Cruse?" asked Angie.

Shawn didn't even know the couple Angie was talking about. "Don't you think we should be working on our project?" she asked.

"Oh, it's okay, you go ahead," Jessica said to her. She turned to Angie. "Josh and Daria are perfect for each other. Wait, wait, you will *never* believe this. Did you hear what happened with them?"

"Yeah, didn't Josh flirt with someone else?" Ashley said.

"Uh-huh! And guess who he flirted *with?*" Angie jumped in.

"Who cares?" Shawn muttered under her breath as she flipped through a few pages in her science textbook.

"Who?" Ashley, Stephanie, and Jessica asked in unison.

Angie looked around, as if to make sure no one who shouldn't be hearing this was around. "Abby Ragonia!" she said slowly.

Everyone—except Shawn—gasped. The librarian looked at the girls and frowned, making a loud *Shush!* noise with her finger pressed to her lips. Shawn, embarrassed, sank lower in her seat.

"Hey, did you guys know that the ancient Egyptians used double pulleys to lift the heavy blocks that made up the pyramids?" Shawn asked, trying to change the subject. She had just read that in her textbook.

Ashley sighed and then grinned. "Like, isn't that new boy, Ashire, from Egypt? He is *sooo* cute!"

"You think everyone is cute!" Stephanie put in.

"So?" Ashley said.

"People—the project?" said Shawn, feeling frustrated.

"Oh, that can wait," said Jessica.

"No, it can't! It's due soon!" Shawn cried. "This is the third time we've met and we still haven't gotten anything done!"

"You'll have time, don't worry," said Ashley.

"Yeah, you're a brain." Stephanie added.

"But it's a *group* project!" Shawn practically yelled.

"Don't worry," Angie assured her. "You're a big part of our group. We couldn't do this without you." She turned back to the other girls. "Listen to *this!* Sara Shimkin told me the most unbelievable thing about Julie Bowen!"

Shawn sighed again. She felt like crying. It was obvious to her that *no one* in her group was going to help on this project. There was so much work to be done, Shawn had no idea how she could ever get it done all by herself.

Late Sunday morning, Amanda, Molly, Natasha, and Peichi met in the Moores' kitchen to work on their science project. The twins' mom walked in and saw them sitting around the table, looking stumped. "No ideas?" she asked.

"We want to do something with cooking," Molly told her. "But so far we can't come up with anything."

"I once heard a chef on TV say something like, 'Cooking is an art. Baking is a science,' " Mom told them. "Why don't you do something on baking?"

Molly jumped up, knocking her chair back behind her. "Yeast!" she cried.

"Yeast?" Amanda asked.

"Yes, the way breads and cakes rise," Molly said.

"Except that it's baking powder, not yeast, that makes cakes rise," Mom interrupted. "Yeast is for making bread rise."

"Cool!" Peichi said. "Doesn't that have something to do with fermentation?"

"I saw something about it in this book," Natasha recalled. She quickly paged through one of the three science books she'd brought. "Here it is," she said, and began to read. "Fermentation is considered one of the earliest forms of biotechnology because a living organism—either a bacterium, a mold, or a yeast—is used to cause a chemical reaction in a food. Around 4000 B.C., Egyptians discovered how to bake leavened bread using yeast."

"What's leavened bread?" Peichi asked.

"It's bread that rises," Natasha said. "Unleavened bread is flat like matzo. It doesn't have any yeast in it."

"This sounds good," Peichi said. "We can have a great science project and taste some yummy cakes and breads while we work on it."

"Too bad Shawn isn't here," Amanda said. "She'd like this project since she *lo-o-o-ves* cakes."

"Actually, Amanda, I think that's *you*," Molly said, poking her sister in the side.

"Okay," Natasha said. "Let's split up the project. We can each do a different part."

"Great idea! I'll be in charge of testing the cake recipes!" Amanda joked. The girls laughed. "Seriously, though," she continued. "What if we work in pairs? One pair can work on bread and yeast, and the other can work on cake and baking powder. Then we can all bake bread and cake here the day before the science fair."

"Good stuff," said Natasha. "But I'd really like to work on the cake part!"

"Me too!" exclaimed Amanda. "Molly and Peichi, is that okay with you guys?"

"Sure, whatever! That sounds fine!" Peichi said with a laugh.

"Great," said Molly. "As long as you save some cake for Peichi and me!" Molly changed the subject. "Hey, I was thinking that if everything goes well with our project today, maybe we can get some things ready for the Barlow party this afternoon. If we make all the cookie dough today, we can keep it in the freezer, and that will be one less thing we have to worry about next Saturday."

Natasha nodded. "That's really smart. I still can't get over how much food we have to make. It's, like, *overwhelming*."

"Yeah," Amanda agreed. "But when we cook next Saturday, we can divide it up like we're doing for the science project. I don't think it will be as bad as it seems right now."

## chapter 8

Peichi, Natasha, and Shawn arrived at the Moores' house about 9:00 in the morning on Saturday, the day of Ms. Barlow's party. Each girl had brought a change of clothes for serving food at the party, and the apron she'd received from Park Terrace Cookware at the end of their summer cooking class.

Molly swung open the door. "Hey! Good morning! I'm so glad you guys are here. Now we can really get going!" she exclaimed. Then she charged back to the kitchen.

"How can she possibly be so awake this early in the morning?" Shawn grumbled as she yawned.

"Probably because we've been up since before seven!" Amanda replied, coming up behind them. "Mom got up early with us so that we could get the turkey in the oven. It will probably be done by eleven o'clock— it's already been in there for two hours. That way, the oven will be free in the afternoon to bake the cookies and the pies. Do you want me to hang up your outfits upstairs? So they don't get all wrinkled?" Amanda asked.

"Sure, that would be great," Peichi replied. "*Mmm*, that turkey smells delicious!"

Peichi, Shawn, and Natasha gave Amanda their outfits and she took them up to the twins' room.

In the kitchen, Mrs. Moore was busy at the sink. "Hi, girls!" she called over her shoulder. "I thought I'd wash all the produce you're using. That way, you won't have to stop once you really get cooking!" Next to the sink sat lots of fresh fruit and vegetables—tiny white mushrooms, large brown portobello mushrooms, garlic, onions, an eggplant, celery, some lemons, green beans, lettuce, tomatoes, green bell peppers, carrots, and about ten green apples! Mrs. Moore had taken the twins shopping at Choice Foods the night before. It wasn't Amanda's favorite way to spend a Friday night, but she agreed with Molly that they would *never* have time to go to the store and get all the food ready on Saturday.

"Wow, thanks *so* much, Mrs. Moore!" Shawn said. "That will be a huge help." She smiled, and Molly caught her eye and smiled back. *Good*, Molly thought, *it seems like everything will be normal today.*

Amanda returned to the kitchen, rolling up her sleeves. "Okay," she said importantly. "Where should we start? Molly?"

Molly grabbed a crumpled piece of paper that was sitting on the counter. "This is the food we'll get completely ready here: the artichoke dip, the hummus and baba ghanouj, the green beans, the chef salad, the wild rice, and the turkey. And the desserts. At Ms. Barlow's, we'll bake the scallops, the stuffed mushrooms, and the baked brie."

"Wait a minute," interrupted Peichi. "Did you ask Ms. Barlow if we could use her oven?"

The twins nodded. "She said it wouldn't be a problem," Amanda added.

"So, what I was thinking," continued Molly, "was that we could start with the appetizers. Then we'll split up, and have some people working on desserts, and some of us working on the main courses. Natasha, do you want to do the hummus and baba ghanouj? Since those are your recipes?"

"Sure," Natasha said.

"Great. Shawn, how about you? Do you want to do the artichoke dip? Or the stuffed mushrooms?"

"I'll do the artichoke dip," Shawn said as she reached for the jars of artichoke hearts.

"Okay. Peichi? How about you?" Molly asked.

"Oh, I'll do the stuffed mushrooms!" Peichi exclaimed. "I love *anything* with stuffing!" The girls laughed.

"So that just leaves Amanda and me," Molly said, turning to her twin. "Do you want—"

"I'll do the baked brie," Amanda said quickly. "Both of them."

Molly sighed. "I guess that leaves me with the scallops," she said. "Gross." Molly *hated* touching raw fish.

"Don't worry, Molls. I'll help with the scallops," Amanda offered. She put on a new CD she had bought a couple days earlier. "Okay, let's get started!"

There was a lot of noise in the kitchen, but not much talking, as everyone got to work. Natasha pricked the eggplant with a long, sharp fork, and then put it in the oven. "If you don't prick some holes in the eggplant before you bake it, it explodes!" she said with a giggle. "Just like baked potatoes!" While the eggplant was roasting along with the turkey, Natasha made the hummus in Mrs. Moore's food processor. She used chick peas, garlic, lemon juice, salt, tahini (a puree of sesame seeds), and a little bit of water. Then she turned on the food processor, and the sharp blade mixed everything together. While the hummus was mixing, Natasha got out the bags of pita bread the twins had bought the night before. Using a sharp knife, she carefully cut the pita bread into neat triangles, and then sealed them in some bags so they wouldn't get stale.

To make the stuffed mushrooms, Peichi first removed the stems from the white mushrooms, then chopped the stems into tiny pieces. She sautéed the chopped mushroom stems, along with chopped carrot, celery, and onion, in some olive oil until the vegetables were tender. Then Peichi added bread crumbs to the vegetable mixture, and then stuffed each of the mushroom caps, placing each stuffed mushroom on a baking tray.

"Done!" cried Peichi. "That was pretty easy. I'm taking these downstairs to the fridge. We'll bake them at Ms. Barlow's house. They're going to taste so good!"

For the artichoke dip, Shawn needed to use the food processor to chop the artichoke hearts, but Natasha was already using it for the hummus. Instead, Shawn measured all the ingredients so she would be ready as soon as Natasha was finished with the food processor. After measuring mayonnaise, sour cream, lemon juice, cornstarch, Parmesan cheese, and minced garlic into a bowl, Shawn opened the jar of artichoke hearts. As soon as Natasha was done with the food processor, Shawn washed it out and dumped the artichoke hearts into the bowl. She quickly clicked the lid into place and turned the food processor on. Suddenly Shawn yelled, and jumped back from the appliance as everyone turned to look at her. Some of the oil the artichoke hearts were stored in was dripping from her face and hair!

"Oh, no!" Mrs. Moore cried. "Shawn, I'm so sorry. I should have warned you—the lid is old, and it doesn't fit as tightly as it used to! If you're not really careful when you put it on, you can get sprayed." Mrs. Moore quickly grabbed a wet towel and helped Shawn wipe the oil out of her hair. "I'm so sorry," Mrs. Moore repeated.

"That's okay," Shawn said. "I don't mind, as long as I don't smell like artichoke hearts all night!"

"Well, if you do, I have some perfume you can borrow," Amanda joked. Shawn smiled at her. "The baked brie is easy!" Amanda commented. "All I had to do was roll out the puff pastry—I used the premade kind—smooth it out with my fingers, spread some mustard on it and wrap the brie wedge in it. For the other one, I put the brie wedge on the pastry, made a slit down the center of the cheese, and then put some sliced apple on it and drizzled some honey on top before I wrapped it up. Then I'll pour some more honey on top before we bake them at Ms. Barlow's."

"Well, at least you don't have to worry about getting brie in your hair!" Shawn teased her as she stirred the artichoke hearts into the other ingredients in the bowl.

"Yeah, but she got some honey in her hair!" Molly said, handing her a wet paper towel.

When Shawn and Amanda were done, they took their appetizers to the downstairs fridge.

"Hurry back so you two can help me with the scallops!" Molly yelled after them. Her appetizer was the most complicated to prepare. She had already sliced some water chestnuts in half, and she was marinating the water chestnuts and scallops in honey and teriyaki sauce for fifteen minutes. Now Molly was struggling to cut strips of bacon in thirds. "The fatty parts are *really* hard to cut through!" she said, exasperated.

"Here, sweetie," said Mrs. Moore. "This knife is sharper than the one you're using—that should make it easier. Just be *very* careful, okay?" She looked at her watch. "I have to drive Matthew to the toy store to get a present for Ben's birthday," she said. "I'll check in as soon as I get home. You girls are really doing a great job!"

"Bye, Mom," said Molly, glancing up quickly at her mother, and then focusing again on cutting the bacon. "Thanks for everything."

Shawn and Amanda stepped in to help Molly. "Okay, what can we do?" Shawn asked.

Molly checked the recipe, and then explained how to assemble the scallops. "Basically, we just have to take a scallop and a water chestnut, hold them together, wrap a piece of bacon around them, and stick a toothpick in the whole thing to secure it," she said. "We won't bake them until we get to Ms. Barlow's house." With three pairs of hands putting together the scallops, they were ready to go into the fridge in no time.

Molly glanced at the clock. "I can't believe it!" she said. "We're done with the appetizers, and it's only 10:30! We *rock!*"

"*And* the turkey will be done really soon, too," Amanda added. "The hard stuff is out of the way."

"Not quite yet," Shawn reminded her. "We still have to do the desserts and stuff."

"Oh, yeah," Amanda remembered. "Well, I'll start the apple crisp right now."

"I'll help you," Shawn quickly volunteered.

"Thanks!" said Amanda.

"The rest of us can work on the cookies and the grapefruit salad," Molly said. She reached into the freezer and pulled out rolls of chocolate chip, gingerbread, and sugar cookie dough that they had prepared last weekend.

Amanda and Shawn got to work peeling all the apples and cutting them into slices that were a quarter of an inch thick. Then they added sugar, cinnamon, nutmeg, lemon juice, and a tiny bit of salt to the apple slices. "This tastes *sooo* good," raved Amanda as she nabbed a slice of spiced apple.

"Hey! No tasting!" Shawn cried, playfully tapping Amanda's hand with a long wooden spoon. The girls giggled. Everyone was having a lot more fun now that the food prep seemed under control. And desserts were *always* fun to make!

The rest of the day zipped by. Mrs. Moore helped the girls take the turkey out of the oven, and she supervised Amanda and Shawn's

work on the apple crisp. Molly steamed
the green beans and tossed them with
sliced almonds, olive oil, and little bit
of fresh garlic. The chopped portobello
mushrooms had been marinating in olive oil, balsamic
vinegar, garlic, oregano, and a little bit of salt for about
an hour. Then Peichi had stir-fried them quickly in olive
oil until they were slightly browned. Natasha had boiled
a package of fresh pasta, and they had tossed the
mushrooms and pasta together, using the extra marinade
as a sauce. All they would need to do at Ms. Barlow's
house is heat up the dish.

"How will we ever get all this stuff over to Ms.
Barlow's?" Amanda asked as she looked down at the
dishes, pots, and pans of food in front of her. There was
food everywhere—on the table, on the oven and the
counters. Mrs. Moore stood with the girls, looking over
all the food.

Amanda glanced at the clock. It was too late for her
to get to Ms. Barlow's early. She'd planned to set up ahead
of the others, so that she could do more than her share
in the beginning. But the cooking had taken so long that
she hadn't been able to get away. At about 2:30, the girls
had stopped for a very quick lunch, eating sandwiches

and chips. Amanda sighed. She'd just have to work extra hard at the party. That would make her feel less guilty about leaving early.

"It all looks wonderful," Mom said. "I think you should pack it in boxes and bring the fancy trays separately. That way, you can arrange it nicely over there. I can drive you over."

"Thanks," Molly said. She turned to Mom. "Do you think it will look fancy enough?"

Mom opened the refrigerator and pulled out a bunch of radishes. "Let me show you something," she said. Taking a small, sharp knife from the drawer, she cut into one of the radishes. When she was done, she had created a red and white rosebud. "We can make a bunch of these and put them alongside the plates as decoration."

"That's what Carmen calls a garnish," Shawn recalled.

"Awesome!" exclaimed Peichi.

Mom showed the girls how to cut the radish rosettes. In a half hour, they had a large bag filled with them. "I have some parsley, too," Mom said. "Sprinkle the parsley around the edges of the platters along with the radishes and it will look first-rate." She glanced at the clock on the wall. "You girls need to go change for the party! It's four-thirty!" Everyone scrambled up the stairs to Molly and Amanda's room.

Amanda reached into the closet and pulled out everyone's outfits. As the other girls started changing, she reached for a dress she had hidden way in the back of the closet, still in a plastic bag from the store. Slowly, she pulled the bag off the dress. She'd been dreaming about wearing this dress all week.

"Amanda! *Ohmygosh!* That dress is *gorgeous!*" Peichi shrieked. Everyone spun around to take a look.

And the dress *was* gorgeous. Made of soft, silky material, the color of the dress changed depending on how the light hit it—sometimes it looked black, sometimes it looked like a rich shade of purple. Best of all, it shimmered whenever Amanda moved. Tiny specks of glitter in the fabric reflected the light. As soon as Amanda tried it on, she knew she had to have it.

"I got it at Lulu's," Amanda told the girls. "It cost almost all the money I have, but I think it was *so* worth it! Molls, zip me up, would you?" She twirled around so her friends could admire the dress some more.

Natasha hung in the doorway, shyly. She wore a white button-down shirt tucked into a plaid skirt. She knew she looked nice, but...plain—especially compared to the other girls in the room. Shawn was wearing a sleeveless, bright green dress made out of crumpled silk, and Peichi had on a long gold skirt with a fuchsia-and-gold top.

"You look nice, Natasha," Amanda said, to be kind.

"Do you think so?" Natasha asked. "I wasn't sure if this was all right to wear—if it was fancy enough."

"No, it looks great," Molly replied. Amanda didn't even hear Natasha's question. She was too busy spraying glitter in her hair.

Once the girls were ready, they all went back down to the kitchen. Molly was the first one in, wearing Amanda's skirt and top. "You look great, Molly," Mom said. "Don't you all look lovely!" she continued. "Before you go, I want to take a picture of you."

"*Oh, no!*" Natasha cried. Everyone turned and saw Natasha standing at the kitchen counter, her white blouse covered in red cranberry juice. The juice had spilled onto the table and was dripping to the floor. "I picked up the bottle of juice by the cap, but it had already been opened and the cap came off in my hand."

She looked at the twins' mom. "I'm so sorry, Mrs. Moore. I'll clean it up." She grabbed a piece of paper towel from the roll on the counter and began mopping up the juice.

"We'll take care of it, Natasha," Molly said. "You have to change that shirt right away!"

"Come on, Natasha," Amanda said. "Let's find you another outfit! I have this purple dress I think would look *great* on you."

"Thanks. Thanks a lot," Natasha said. "I'm really, really sorry."

"Don't worry about it," Mom said as she began wiping the table. "Natasha, go into the bathroom and run cold water over your blouse right away. Amanda, you can bring the dress to her there." Natasha grabbed her backpack and dashed up the stairs and into the twins' bathroom as Amanda followed up after her.

"Thanks for letting us have the sleepover here for New Year's," Peichi said to Mrs. Moore while they waited for the two girls to get back. "I think it's going to be awesome."

"You're welcome," Mrs. Moore said with a smile.

"Is Natasha coming this time?" Shawn asked.

Molly frowned. "I don't think so," she said. "Her mom still doesn't let her go to sleepover parties."

"No sleepovers!" Peichi cried. "That is *such* a bummer!"

"I wonder if it would help if I called her mother," Mom offered. "I think I'll ask Natasha if she'd like me to do that."

Just then, Amanda and Natasha reappeared. Amanda led the way into the kitchen, while Natasha hung back shyly.

"Doesn't she look *great?*" Amanda asked proudly.

"Wow, Natasha, you do look great!" said Shawn.

Natasha smiled and said, "Thanks. This dress is *so* pretty. Thanks for letting me borrow it, Amanda! I promise I won't spill anything else tonight!" The girls laughed, and then Molly cleared her throat.

"Well," Molly said, "it's time to take all this food over to Ms. Barlow's!"

## chapter 9

Soon all the food was packed, and Mom drove them to Ms. Barlow's in her big, old car. Amanda thought it was the most embarrassing car on earth. Mom loved it because she'd inherited it from her Aunt Hazel. The car didn't bother Molly, but Amanda wished she would just drive a nice SUV like the other mothers in Park Terrace. Still, the girls were grateful for the ride. Ms. Barlow had promised to call them a car service to take them back home after the party.

Mom drove the few blocks to Ms. Barlow's house and pulled up to the curb in front. "A parking spot right in front," she said. "Unbelievable!"

"Awesome luck," Molly agreed.

Amanda nodded but didn't say anything. In fact, she hadn't spoken for the last ten minutes. As they grew closer to the actual event, she'd begun feeling more and more guilty about what she planned to do. No matter how many times she told herself that she would make it up to her friends by working extra hard, it still *felt* wrong.

"Well, girls," said Mom, "I think you all better get moving, don't you?"

"Guess so," said Molly. "Wish us luck!"

"I don't think you'll need it tonight—you've already got everything under control! Have fun!" said Mom as she hugged first Molly, then Amanda.

"Thanks!" said Shawn, Peichi, and Natasha, waving good-bye to Mrs. Moore as she pulled out of sight.

"All done with setting up!" Molly said as she plopped onto a kitchen chair.

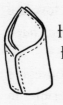"Finally!" said Natasha, fanning herself with the edge of a tablecloth. "There are cloths on all the tables. The glasses and silverware are out. The napkins are all folded and laid out. Salt and pepper shakers are all full."

Peichi came in. "Okay. The punch is on the table. The ice bucket is next to it. *Oops!* I forgot to put the ladle in the punch." She grabbed the ladle from the counter and hurried back out with it.

"What a ton of work!" Natasha said.

"We can't stop now, we aren't nearly done!" said Shawn. "The appetizers have to go into the oven. The platters have to be set out and garnished. The salads have to be tossed. We have to put little bowls of dressing next to the salads. The main courses have to be reheated and arranged on platters."

"Don't worry," Amanda said brightly as she hurried in. "I have everything under control. You all take a little rest." She picked up a tray of the stuffed mushrooms and slid them into the oven on the shelf under the scallops. "How can I brown the top of the mushrooms if the scallops need to be browned, too?" she wondered aloud. "I know. I'll just broil the mushrooms for a couple minutes after the scallops are done." Then she pulled out the bowl of artichoke dip. "I'll microwave this for a couple of minutes as soon as the first guest arrives. Then it will be warm and we won't have to worry about using the oven any more than we absolutely have to."

"Wow! It's super-caterer girl," Shawn teased Amanda.

Normally, Amanda would have laughed and struck a Supergirl pose. But her guilty conscience made her turn away, mumbling, "I just want to do my part."

Shawn gazed at Molly and Natasha with an expression that asked, *Did I say something wrong?*

Molly could only shrug back at her. She had the feeling that something was up with Amanda, but she couldn't figure out what it might be. Maybe she was just staying super-busy to keep her mind off of Connor's party.

Ms. Barlow swooped into the kitchen wearing a long, red, silky bathrobe with lace trim. On her feet were black high-heeled mules trimmed with feathers. Her hair was rolled in electric curlers, but her makeup was finished and she was wearing a *ton* of perfume. "It smells *divine* in here," she said. "Is everything under control?"

"Totally under control," Amanda assured her.

Ms. Barlow looked her up and down. "Oh, don't you look *gorgeous*, Amanda."

"Thanks," Amanda said. "You look really pretty, too."

"Oh, you *all* look lovely, girls," Ms. Barlow said. "My guests will arrive in another fifteen minutes or so. Let them mingle for about ten minutes and then start with the appetizers."

"Sure thing," Shawn told her.

Ms. Barlow clutched her headful of curlers. "Good heavens! I thought I'd taken these out already! I'd better dash upstairs right away, right away!" She hurried out of the room, her long robe flapping behind her.

Natasha giggled. "Wouldn't it be funny if she'd forgotten the curlers altogether and wore them all night?"

"How embarrassing," Shawn said with a little laugh. She stood and stretched. "I just got a second blast of energy. I'll start putting the main dishes on platters," she said.

"I'll set out the garnishes on each platter," Natasha volunteered.

"I already garnished the platters," Amanda said. "I've set a serving spoon beside each one and I've put the salads into bowls."

"You'd better slow down, Amanda," Peichi said as she returned to the kitchen. "You're going to be exhausted by the time this is over."

"You might be right," Amanda said. She clutched her throat. "I am starting to feel a little funny."

"Then sit down and chill for a minute," Peichi advised her.

This was it. Amanda's plan was about to begin. "Yes," she said in a small, weak voice. "Maybe I should sit for a minute."

Amanda stood in the middle of Ms. Barlow's crowded living room. She held a tray of artichoke dip surrounded by small pieces of toasted sourdough bread. "Artichoke dip?" she offered a man in a black suit.

"Don't mind if I do," the man said. Amanda handed him a napkin, and he plucked a piece of bread from the tray.

Amanda dashed away before the man could get some artichoke dip on his bread. She'd spotted Molly walking into the room with a newly filled punch bowl.

"Molls," she croaked in the scratchiest voice she could put on. "Molls, I have to talk to you."

Molly set the bowl on the table. "What's wrong with your voice?" she asked. She hooked her hand onto

Amanda's arm and drew her into the kitchen. "What's wrong, Manda?"

Amanda pointed to her throat. "Can hardly talk," she said in a scratchy whisper. "Throat really sore. Can't swallow."

Peichi joined them, balancing an empty tray in her right hand. "Everyone *loves* these scallops! This is the third time I've refilled this tray! We're going to run out." Then she noticed the sick look on Amanda's face. "Whoa—what's the matter?"

"Amanda's throat is super sore," Molly told her.

"Didn't I say you were going to get sick?" Peichi reminded Amanda. "You'd better go home. You're going to make yourself sicker and get everyone else sick if you stay. And you don't want to be sick for Christmas!"

"You should totally go home," Molly agreed.

Amanda shook her head. "Too much work to do."

"We can handle it," Peichi assured her. Just then, Shawn came in the kitchen.

"What's up, Chef Girls?" Shawn asked. "You guys need to get back out there. Natasha and I can't handle it all by ourselves!"

Molly shook her head. "Amanda has to go home. She's sick."

Shawn looked at Amanda sympathetically. "That's rotten, Manda! Do you want me to make you a cup of tea?"

"No, I just want to go home to bed," Amanda said sadly. It took all her acting skills to keep looking sick and sad when she wanted to shout for joy. Her plan was working! "Thanks for being so understanding, you guys." She smiled weakly at her friends.

Amanda took a step toward the closet for her coat. Molly suddenly reached out and clasped her wrist. "Wait! You can't go! You're not allowed to walk home alone at night," Molly said. "I'll call Mom or Dad to come get you." She hurried into the kitchen to use the phone.

*Oh, no!* thought Amanda. She hadn't planned for this. For a moment, she really *did* feel sick!

**A**manda sat in a chair at the kitchen table and checked the clock on stove. It was 7:45. Connor's party had started at 5:00. All the kids had to be back from skating by now. The most awesome party of the entire holiday season—her best chance to hang out with Justin—was passing her by while she sat there.

Suddenly the kitchen door swung open. "Okay, I'm going to try calling again," Molly said, picking up the cordless phone and punching in the twins' phone number. "Somebody's *still* on the Internet!" she complained. "I can't get through. And I tried Mom and Dad's cell phone numbers, but no one picks up. Maybe Ms. Barlow can call you a car service now."

"No, I don't want to bother her in the middle of the party." She held her throat and slowly stood. "I can walk home alone. I'll be fine. Really."

"I should go with you," Molly said. She looked around the room with a worried expression. "But if we both leave there will be *way* too much work."

"I'll be fine. Really," Amanda assured her.

"I guess it will be all right," Molly gave in. "Call me as soon as you get home."

Amanda nodded and took a step toward the door. She held her hand up in a little wave, which Molly returned. It took all her self-control not to dash for the door. Instead, she forced herself to walk slowly to the hall closet and put on her coat.

Molly stood, watching Amanda. Her eyes were filled with concern.

*Don't look at me like that!* thought Amanda. She felt so guilty.

Finally, she made her way out the front door. It was a cold, clear night. Amanda breathed in the freezing air and was suddenly charged with new energy.

Connor's house was only three blocks away. Amanda headed there in a brisk half-run. By the time she arrived, she was breathless. The house was lit from within. Through the front window she could see kids working on the Christmas tree that reached all the way to the top of the ten-foot ceiling. Music and laughter floated out into the street.

She smoothed her hair and pulled a little jar of lip gloss out of her purse. After heading through the iron gate and up the front steps, Amanda rang the doorbell and waited. In a few moments, Connor opened the door. "Hey, Amanda. Come on in. Where's Molly?"

"Oh, Dish had a big job tonight, but they didn't need me. Everything was under control, so I came over," Amanda said with a big smile.

"Cool," he said. "I mean, it's too bad they couldn't make it, but I'm glad you could. There's food on the table over there and ornaments are in the box by the tree. You can hang your coat in the closet over there."

"Thanks," she said as Connor headed back to the tree. Looking around, the first thing Amanda saw was that her dress was *way* too fancy for this party. *What a dummy*, she scolded herself. She should have realized everyone would be dressed for skating. She suddenly wished she had a change of clothes.

Omar was on his way to the food table. "Hi, Amanda," he said. "Hey, you look really nice. But why are you all dressed up?"

"I just came from a Dish job," she said. "We had to cater this fancy party, so we had to serve the guests and everything. We had to look nice really nice like the other guests so we wouldn't stand out."

"A career woman," Omar said. "I'm impressed. Very cool."

Amanda smiled at him. "I'm going to hang up my coat. See ya," she said, moving toward the coat closet. Now that she had an excuse prepared for why she was so dressed up, she felt a little better.

She hung up her coat and stood in the hallway, looking around. It felt strange to be on her own. Most of the time her friends were around. At the very least, she always had Molly to talk to. *Where's Justin?* she wondered.

She went into the living room, where kids were decorating the beautiful tree. She dug into the ornament box and pulled out a pack of silver tinsel. Tearing open the top, she began pulling out the long, silver strands and laying them on the branches.

All around her, kids talked to one another, joking and laughing. "It's a beautiful tree," she said to a girl beside her.

The girl turned and nodded. "Yes, it is," she agreed. Then she saw a friend of hers and walked away. Amanda sighed. Even trimming a tree wasn't much fun when you felt all alone. At least it gave her something to do other than stand there and look uncomfortable.

She spread the tinsel on the tree for another fifteen minutes. Then she spotted Justin! Her heartbeat sped up. He looked as cute as ever, wearing a bulky black knit sweater and baggy jeans. He noticed her and smiled. She waved and he headed in her direction.

"Hey, Amanda!"

"Hey!" she said, smiling. "How was the skating? I couldn't make it to that part of the party."

"It was great," he replied. "I love skating at night. We ruled the whole rink. And Connor's mom makes the best hot chocolate. You should try some!"

"Awesome!" Amanda said brightly. This was so great! Suddenly, everything she'd done to get here seemed totally worth it! "I love skating, too. I would have gone but Dish had a big job tonight. Luckily I was able to get out and—"

"Hey! Justin, my man! Was skating ragin' or what?" Chris Ratner held his hand out for a high-five.

"It totally rocked!" Justin agreed, slapping Chris's outstretched palm. "Did you see when Josh Cruse spun off into the wall?" Justin waved "bye" to Amanda over his shoulder as he and Chris walked away.

A quick tap on her shoulder made Amanda turn.

It was Angie.

"So, you have a huge crush on Justin," Angie said nastily. "You make it pretty obvious, don't you?"

Amanda could only stare at her. Angie had totally taken her by surprise. No one but her friends knew how she felt about Justin.

*There's only one possible explanation*, Amanda told herself. *Shawn blabbed!* "You're crazy," Amanda mumbled as she turned away from Angie.

"Yeah, like I'm the crazy one," Angie said as Amanda walked away. "At least I didn't come to a skating party dressed for a prom."

Why had she ever thought this party was going to be so great? It might have been fun if Molly were with her. How could she have left them all to work at Ms. Barlow's just to come to this party? What was she even thinking?

Amanda's stomach churned. She was having such a miserable time that she was actually starting to feel sick.

The only thing to do now was to get out of there—and *fast!* If she hurried straight home, she could be in bed by the time Molly got back. She rushed to the coat closet, grabbed her coat, and pulled it on as she went toward the door.

As she yanked open the door, she stood face to face with a girl entering the party.

It was Molly!

**B**oth twins jumped back in surprise.

"I thought you were sick!" Molly cried.

Peichi, Natasha, and Shawn hurried up the front steps behind Molly. Together, the four girls stepped into the front hall and faced Amanda.

"I can't believe you pretended to be sick to get out of helping with Dish," Shawn said coldly. Angie waved from the living room and Shawn, turning her back on Amanda, hurried off to join her.

Amanda opened her mouth to speak, but no sound came out. After all, what could she say?

Peichi stepped up to Amanda. Her mouth had dropped open in surprise. She just shook her head, as if she were too shocked to speak. Then she passed Amanda, saying nothing. Amanda turned to Natasha, but she only turned her head away and followed Peichi.

Amanda and Molly stood together by the door. "Why aren't you still over at Ms. Barlow's?" Amanda dared to ask.

"Once we were done setting up the main dishes, Ms. Barlow said she didn't need us anymore," Molly explained.

"She said her cleaning lady was coming tomorrow and she'd clean up."

"Oh," Amanda said. "I wonder why she didn't tell us that in the beginning."

"Don't change the subject!" Molly said angrily. "I thought you were sick. What are you doing here?"

Amanda's eyes filled with tears. Molly looked so angry and disappointed in her.

Molly whirled around and flung the door open. "Where are you going?" Amanda asked as Molly stomped down the front steps. "Molly, come back!"

She ran down the steps after her. "Wait!" she called, but Molly kept going. "Molly, please," Amanda shouted after her.

Molly stopped and turned toward Amanda. "You are so selfish, Amanda!" she shouted. "Do you even have any idea how selfish you are? It's disgusting. All you care about is yourself and your clothes! No one else even matters to you! And you know what? You've always been selfish. But ever since you were in that stupid play, it's been completely unbearable!"

"Don't shout, Molly," Amanda said. "We're out in the street. It's embarrassing."

"Embarrassing?" Molly continued shouting. "Do you want to know what's embarrassing? Having you as a sister embarrasses *me!*" She hurried on down the street.

Amanda ran to keep up with her. "Try to understand," she pleaded. "I worked extra hard in the beginning of the party so that it would be fair when I left early."

"*Fair?*" Molly yelled. "Only *you* would think that way. That's not how it works, Amanda! You don't just get to decide when you work in a business. We all do it together. Everybody else wanted to go to Connor's party, but we knew we had to do the job. Why do you think you're more special than the rest of us? Not to mention that *you* got everyone into the catering job without even asking! I'm stuck with you as my sister, but I don't even know *why* everyone else puts up with it. Actually, Shawn seems pretty sick of you, too. So I hope you're happy with yourself."

Amanda stopped, stung. "Molly—" she began. "Molly, that was really mean. Would you just *talk* to me for a minute?"

Molly wouldn't even turn around to look at her.

When they arrived home, the house was dark. Amanda found a note on the refrigerator. "Dad and I have gone to the movies. Matthew is at the Baders' house. Hope everything went okay with the party! Love, Mom."

*Thank goodness*, Amanda thought. If her parents were home, they would want to know why the girls were fighting. Amanda heard Molly going upstairs and went to follow her up. Before she reached the top landing, she heard the bathroom door slam.

With a sigh, Amanda continued on to their bedroom and threw herself on her bed. Was it all true? Was she really that selfish? Did she really embarrass Molly? Was it her fault that Shawn didn't hang out with them very much anymore?

A high-pitched shriek made Amanda sit upright. It was Molly! Amanda bolted off the bed and ran to the bathroom.

"Molly! What's wrong? Open the door!" Amanda yelled, pounding on the door.

The door slowly swung open. Molly stood holding a pretty journal. She looked stunned and upset.

"What?" Amanda asked.

Molly held the book out to her. "This," she said simply. "It's Natasha's journal. She must have dropped it when she was changing her outfit earlier. It must have fallen out of her bag. I found it lying open on the floor."

"Oh, wow," Amanda said. "You didn't read it, did you?"

Molly nodded. "I only read the page that was open. I didn't realize what it was at first. Amanda...would you do me a favor? Please?"

"Sure. What?" Amanda was eager to do something for Molly—anything to smooth things over.

"Would you read this?"

"I can't!" Amanda gasped. "It isn't right!"

"Please," Molly pleaded. "Just read the same page I

read. I need to talk to you about it. I can't handle it by myself. This is really serious."

Amanda took the journal from Molly and slowly began to read the last page.

> *I acted like such a jerk today. Peichi's new neighbors must think I'm a total nutcase. I was rude to Molly, too. She was only trying to be nice. But how can I ever explain to my friends what's really bothering me? It's something I just don't know how to talk about. And my mom would freak out if she knew I was talking about it.*
>
> *But I can't stand living a lie anymore. In some ways, I want to tell them the truth, but I'm afraid. They might think differently of me if they knew. I just want to fit in and be like other kids. Why do I have to be different!? It's not fair! Keeping this secret is driving me crazy.*

Amanda looked up when she'd finished reading. "Oh, wow," she said, exhaling. Amanda didn't even realize she had been holding her breath. "What do you think she's hiding from us?" she asked.

Molly threw her arms wide. "I have no idea! It sounds awful, though. I feel so sorry for her. What should we do?"

"What *can* we do?" Amanda questioned. "It's not

like we can just go up to Natasha and say, 'We read your journal. What's the big secret that's driving you insane?'"

"I know. She'd hate us for reading her journal," Molly agreed.

"Listen, Molly. I'm really, really, really sorry about what I did," Amanda began. "I told myself it wasn't that big a deal, that I'd make it up to you by working hard—but lying to you and the others was rotten."

"It was super-rotten," Molly agreed. "I was so worried about you walking home at night and feeling so sick. I was only going to Connor's party to tell him I couldn't stay. I wouldn't have had fun at the party until I knew you were okay."

"Thanks," Amanda said. "Are you still mad at me?"

"Yes!" Molly said. "I haven't forgiven you. I feel like I can't even trust you, Amanda. I still can't believe you would lie to me. You're my *twin*."

Tears stung Amanda's eyes. "I know, Molly. I'm so, so sorry."

Amanda sighed and rolled over in bed. The room was dark, but she could hear Molly breathing deeply as she slept. It was a comforting sound, really. It reminded her how lucky she felt to be a twin—especially to be Molly's twin.

Amelia and Amanda. Molly and Mandy. They could have called themselves those names. But they had made their names sound different to help people tell them apart. Right now, though, Amanda didn't want to be apart from Molly. She was truly sorry she'd done anything to hurt their closeness. Molly had calmed down some. She wasn't as angry as she had been. But her anger was replaced by something even worse.

Betrayal and distrust.

Amanda pulled her knees to her chest and sat there in the dark, thinking. She was lucky not only to have Molly, but also Shawn and Peichi. Even Natasha was becoming a close friend. How could she have taken their friendships for granted like that?

Throwing back her covers, Amanda got out of bed. Silently, she padded her way downstairs to the computer. She turned it on and logged on to the Internet.

**To:** happyface, qtpie490, BrooklynNatasha
**From:** Mooretimes2
**Date:** 12/17, 1:56 AM
**Re:** Sincerely, Xtremely, Sorry

───────────────────────

Hi! Amanda here. Wait! Don't turn off your computer until you read what I have to say. Please!

If I were you, I'd hate me, too.
Please don't hate me, though. Lying to
you guys tonight was a terrible thing.
Friends don't lie to one another. You
can't trust a person who lies to you.
I want you all to be able to trust me
like I trust you. I really want to
make this up to you guys. Please
forgive me and give me another chance.
You won't be sorry.
    Love,
    Amanda ☹

Amanda hit SEND, then sighed again as she turned off the computer. Even though it was late at night, she was wide awake. She didn't think she'd be able to sleep at all. Every time she closed her eyes, she remembered the looks on her friends' faces when they saw her at Connor's party—first surprised, then confused, then mad. Amanda went into the kitchen to make herself some hot chocolate, and then she curled up on the couch with a blanket. Maybe she'd be able to fall asleep if she watched some TV. At the very least, it might take her mind off of the terrible evening she'd had.

## chapter 12

"Hi Molly! Hi Amanda! Oh, it's so great to see you!" said Carmen Piccolo. Her reddish-blond hair was swept up into a messy bun, and she was already wearing her apron. "Come in! Come in!"

Molly and Amanda smiled at her. It was good to be back in the kitchen of Park Terrace Cookware. They'd had so much fun learning to cook there. They sat at one of the long tables—the one next to the sink.

Amanda was surprised that Carmen even recognized her. She couldn't possibly look like her usual self—not after the terrible night she'd had. Amanda felt like she had barely gotten any sleep the night before. She had watched an old movie called *It's a Wonderful Life* and then fell asleep on the couch.

This morning she'd slept until nearly 9:45 until Molly shook her awake. Then she'd bolted out the door in an old, faded sweatshirt and jeans that already had flour spilled on them from cooking for Ms. Barlow's party. She hadn't even had time to shower or brush her hair, so she'd just thrown it into a loose ponytail. The ends were sticking out at all angles. *I must look like such a mess,* Amanda thought. But she just wasn't in the mood to care.

Shawn and Peichi came in, laughing about something. Their smiles faded when they spotted Amanda. But then their expressions softened and they waved.

Amanda felt a rush of hopefulness. Maybe they'd read her e-mail. *Maybe* they'd forgiven her. She crossed her fingers and hoped so.

Peichi and Shawn sat at the same table as the twins. They both sat closer to Molly than to Amanda. It was as if they needed to warm up slowly to the idea of being friendly with Amanda again.

"*Hello* everybody!" said a young man with a twinkle in his dark eyes. Freddie Gonzalez was Carmen's assistant. "Are you ready to make some *swee-ee-eet* gingerbread houses?"

"Only if we can gobble 'em up," said Omar as he came into the room with Connor behind him. Another boy followed them in, too.

"*Justin!*" Amanda whispered to Molly. What was he doing there? She looked awful!

Connor introduced Justin to Carmen. "Hey, Carmen, this is our buddy Justin. We told him about getting to eat all the awesome things that we make in class and he wanted to come. Is that okay?"

"I always welcome a new chef. Hi, Justin," Carmen greeted him.

Natasha was the last to come in. She sat beside Peichi, but smiled at Molly and Amanda.

Soon the class was busy making the gingerbread dough. They combined flour, baking powder, ground ginger, ground cinnamon, ground cloves, and salt in a huge bowl. Then they beat in butter and brown sugar with the electric mixer.

It was hard for the Chef Girls to stay angry with Amanda when they were all laughing and covered in flour.

Next came eggs, molasses, and water. Dough splattered all of them when Omar turned on the electric mixer before he put it into the bowl. Amanda forgot all about her looks as she giggled and ducked the spray.

"*Eww!*" Peichi squealed. "Watch it, Omar!"

"*Eww!*" Omar imitated Peichi.

"Clean-up time!" Carmen sang out when the dough mixture was done. "We have to let it set a while. We won't be bored, though. After we wash up, I'll show you how to map out your house pieces on grid paper and make a pattern."

"Is it like sewing a dress?" Natasha asked.

"A lot like that, yes," Carmen replied.

This session of the class was much quieter than the last one had been. It required serious thought and planning. Shawn watched Molly, Amanda, Natasha, and Peichi trace out their pieces. She couldn't imagine Angie and her crew giving any project this much attention. The two groups sure were very different.

"Lunch!" Carmen announced at noon.

"You're in for a treat," Freddie told them. "I have prepared my special *Pastelon de Carne.*" He opened the oven door and slid out a tray.

"Meat pies!" Omar cried. "Yum."

As the others ate, Molly took Amanda aside. "We should return Natasha's journal to her," she said. Amanda nodded. Neither of them was looking forward to this. Natasha might suspect they'd read it—and she'd be right. Even though they'd only read one page, they still felt guilty about it. Actually, they felt both guilty and worried. What was the terrible secret Natasha was hiding? And how could they try to help her with it if she wouldn't tell them?

"Natasha," Molly called. "Can you come here a sec?"

As Natasha walked over, Molly fished the journal from her bag. "You left this at our house last night," Molly said, handing her the journal.

Natasha's eyes widened, and her neck turned red.

"How did you know it was mine?" she asked.

Molly and Amanda exchanged a quick, nervous glance. "Your name is on the front," Amanda said.

"No, it isn't," Natasha said, staring down at the journal.

Molly laughed uncomfortably. "Oh, it was easy to figure out that it belonged to you. It wasn't mine and it didn't belong to Amanda, and you were the only other person in the upstairs bathroom that day. So...we just figured it had to be yours."

*Way to go, Molls!* Amanda thought.

"That makes sense. Thanks," Natasha said. "I was going crazy looking for it this morning!" Natasha carefully tucked the journal into her backpack.

"No problem," Molly said.

Amanda grabbed Molly's wrist and gave it a little squeeze. "Thank goodness that's over," she said.

"Definitely."

After lunch, they rolled the dough flat and sprinkled it with flour. Then they laid out their pattern pieces. Carmen and Freddie helped them cut the pieces using sharp knives. Carmen collected the scraps of dough and put them in a big silver bowl. "We can make gingerbread cookies with these," she explained.

"All right!" Omar and Connor cheered.

It took only fifteen minutes until the house pieces were baked to a golden brown. While the pieces were cooling, Carmen helped them make icing. "Make a lot," she instructed. "The icing is for decorating and for gluing the pieces together."

They spent the rest of the class building the houses. It was tricky. The houses wouldn't always stand up straight. Luckily, Carmen and Freddie had lots of tricks for making them stand the way they were supposed to. The best part was after all the houses were constructed. Carmen and Freddie brought out *huge* bags of candy for the kids to use to decorate their gingerbread houses. Candy canes, peppermint drops, chocolate candies, peanut butter cups, gumdrops...it looked like Halloween!

"Hey man, slow down!" said Freddie with a laugh as Omar pretended to pounce on the candy. "Make sure everyone gets enough candy to decorate their houses before you eat any 'extra' pieces!"

By about four o'clock, the class stood among a town of beautifully decorated gingerbread houses. "Awesome," Omar said. "These look *way* too good to eat, though."

"Not to worry!" Carmen said. "I whipped these together while you guys were busy decorating your houses." She lifted a tray of gingerbread girls and boys. Each had a name written on it in icing. "One for each of you," she said. "There's milk and juice in the fridge."

Molly and Amanda laughed with delight when they saw that their two cookies were alike—except Molly's wore a high ponytail and Amanda's wore her hair in a flip. In fact, each cookie had a small detail in the decoration that was like the person it was intended for.

The girls sat and ate their gingerbread cookies. The fun of the day had brought them back together again. They were all feeling tired but happy. "Tomorrow night is the first night of Hanukkah," Natasha reminded them. "Are all you guys still coming?"

"Of course!" Amanda said quickly. "I mean...I am, if I'm still invited."

"You are," said Natasha with a little smile. Everyone else told her they were coming, too.

"That's great. You don't have to get all dressed up, but just sort of look...neat," Natasha said happily.

"I can do neat," Shawn said.

"Definitely," Peichi agreed.

"If we're all going to be busy tomorrow night, we'd better get going on our science project. It's due this Wednesday," Molly reminded them. "We still have to finish our poster."

Shawn sighed.

"What's wrong?" Amanda asked her.

"Oh, nothing," she said. "My group still has a lot of work to do on our project." She didn't want to tell them the whole truth. The *whole* truth was that *she* had a lot of work to do, since she was the only one doing *any* work in her group. "I'd better get going," Shawn said, popping the rest of her cookie into her mouth.

"Why? No one else is leaving yet. Stay a couple more

minutes!" Amanda encouraged. But Shawn just shook her head.

"No, I can't. I have a lot of stuff going on," Shawn said. She waved good-bye to her friends and went to say good-bye to Carmen and Freddie.

Amanda sat back and sighed. It seemed clear to her that Shawn didn't want to spend any more time with her than she had to. Was Molly right? Had she really been so selfish that she had driven Shawn away?

## chapter 13

"What are you baking?" Molly asked Amanda. She'd just gotten home from her tutoring session with Athena, and something in the kitchen smelled *wonderful.*

"Mandelbrodt," Amanda replied.

"Mandel*what?*" Molly said.

"It's a dessert. Like a cookie. It reminds me of the Italian cookie called biscotti. I found a recipe for mandelbrodt on the Internet. It's for us to bring to Natasha's tonight. From all the Chef Girls."

Molly sat at the kitchen table. "I can't stop thinking about Natasha's diary."

"Me neither," Amanda agreed. "When we go there tonight, maybe we'll be able to figure out what her problem could be. We could get Peichi and Shawn to look around, too."

"I'm not sure we should tell them about it," Molly said. "After all, we're not even supposed to know."

"But it's for Natasha's own good, so we can help her," Amanda said. "Just like how you wanted me to read the diary, too."

"I know, but it doesn't feel right to me," Molly insisted.

"Maybe you're right," Amanda finally agreed. "We'll keep it between you and me. Secrets are so weird," she continued with a sigh. "Most of the time they just cause trouble, but sometimes you just have to keep secrets."

"Why is everything so complicated?" Molly asked.

"I don't know. I guess it just is," Amanda replied.

The timer on top of the oven rang. "It's done!" Amanda said excitedly. She pulled out the cookie sheet.

"It smells great!" Molly said.

"I hope it tastes as good as it smells," said Amanda.

Molly looked at the loaves that Amanda had just taken out of the oven. "Those look more like cakes than cookies," Molly commented.

"Well, as soon as it cools a little, I'm going to slice it up," Amanda told her.

"Was it hard to make?" Molly said, taking a whiff of the mandelbrodt.

Amanda shook her head. "It was simple. I just mixed some flour, eggs, sugar, shortening, baking powder, a bit of salt, and some vanilla together. The recipe said you could add either chopped nuts or chocolate chips."

"And let me guess," Molly said with a laugh. "You added the chips!"

"Exactly!" Amanda replied.

Amanda sliced up the mandelbrodt and then pulled a

colorful cookie tin with snowflakes on it from a bag. "I bought this at Park Terrace Cookware this afternoon. Isn't it cute? I'm going to put the mandelbrodt into it. The recipe said it will keep a really long time if you put it in a tin."

"Hmmm," Molly murmured. "There are eight days of Hanukkah. We can add mandelbrodt to our menu for this week if we get any last-minute orders."

Amanda gave her a high five.

"Oh, we'd better get going," Molly said, looking at her watch. "We're supposed to be there by sundown. These days the sun is setting by five o'clock."

The girls ran upstairs to change. "Do I look neat enough?" Molly asked. She had re-done her ponytail and put on her nicest blue turtleneck. She'd even put on a pair of black flared pants instead of her usual jeans.

"Very neat," Amanda said. She looked a bit dressier, wearing a short blue pleated skirt and a long black ribbed sweater. She twirled once. "Am I okay?"

"Mrs. Ross will probably think your skirt is too short," Molly said.

Amanda put her hands on her hips. "Well, I'm not going out in public looking all out of style just because Mrs. Ross might not approve," she said. But then she remembered how Molly had scolded her for being selfish and only caring about clothing. "Oh, whatever," she said with a sigh. She pulled a long skirt from her closet. "This is just as good, I suppose," she grumbled. "And it will look cool with my new boots."

"What new boots?" Molly asked.

"The ones Mom and Dad got me for Christmas. I found them in the front hall closet."

"You can't wear those!" Molly cried. "It will spoil the surprise for them."

Amanda sulked. "They won't see them."

"Manda," Molly said in a warning tone.

"Oh, you're no fun," Amanda complained. "Sorry, you're right," she added quickly. "I'm kidding. All right. I won't wear them. I can't wait for Christmas, though. Those boots are really awesome."

By 4:45 they were headed for Natasha's house. The pink light of sunset bounced off the icy sidewalk. They heard the sound of footsteps behind them and turned. Peichi was running to catch up with them.

"What's in the tin?" she asked as they walked together.

"Mandelbrodt," Amanda told her. "I made it myself. It's from all of us."

"That was really nice of you," Peichi said.

Amanda smiled. Peichi had said just the right thing. Amanda had decided she was going to change her image from selfish to sweet and thoughtful. It was more than that, though. She really didn't want to be selfish. She actually wanted to *become* sweet and thoughtful—although she wasn't entirely sure it was in her nature. Still, she figured that if she really tried, she could be a lot more considerate of the people around her.

When they got to the Rosses' house, Natasha let them in. Shawn was already there. She smiled and seemed very happy that they'd arrived. Even though Shawn was always cool around adults, it must have been kind of awkward for her to sit and chat with the Rosses in the formal living room.

Mrs. Ross got up to greet them. "Hello, girls. We're so glad you could come."

Amanda presented her tin. "We made some mandel-brodt. It's from all the Chef Girls. Happy Hanukkah!"

Mr. Ross stood and reached for the tin. "Mandelbrodt! My favorite!"

Mrs. Ross put up her hand to stop him. "Not until after dinner!"

"Then let's get started so we can eat!" he said with a smile. He waved them into the living room. "Come!"

The menorah with its nine candleholders stood on the coffee table. "I thought there were eight candles," Molly wondered, "for the eight nights of Hanukkah."

"There are," Natasha said. "The ninth candle is called the Shamash. It's used to light the others."

The girls found seats on the couches and chairs around the menorah. "I'd like to start tonight by reading the story of the Maccabees," Mr. Ross said.

He put on his glasses and picked up a book from the table. He read about the Maccabees trying to restore their holy temple, which had been destroyed in a war against the Syrians. They had only a little oil with which to light their lamp, but it lasted for the eight nights that they needed to work. It was a miracle!

Mrs. Ross got up and took the Shamash candle from the menorah. Mr. Ross lit it. "Natasha," Mrs. Ross said, "since your friends are here tonight, why don't you light the first candle?"

Natasha took the lit candle from her mother and lit the first candle on the menorah. As she did it, she said three prayers in Hebrew.

When the candle lighting was finished, they all sat at the Rosses' big dining room table. It was set with the family's best china dishware and sterling silver forks and knives.

"I hope you're all hungry, because I made a big dinner," Mrs. Ross said as everyone sat down at the table.

"Oh, we are," Amanda said. "*Very* hungry!"

"Good! I've made roast chicken and latkes and all sorts of things."

"Latkes?" asked Peichi.

"They're potato pancakes,"

Natasha explained. "They're a traditional Hanukkah dish."

"What other kinds of food do you eat during Hanukkah?" Shawn asked.

"A lot of fried food!" Natasha said.

"Why's that?" Amanda asked.

"Well, oil played a big part in the Hanukkah story—with it lasting for eight days instead of just one," Natasha explained.

By the end of the meal, everyone was laughing and talking at once. For dessert, they had *sufganiyot*—jelly filled donuts. And when they thought they couldn't eat another bite, Mr. Ross gave the girls some Hanukkah gelt—little chocolate coins wrapped in gold paper.

Natasha sat at the dining room table and looked around at her parents and her friends. *This was a perfect way to spend the first night of Hanukkah*, she thought. She hoped this feeling would last forever. But deep down, she knew it could not.

"The judges are coming to us," Molly told Amanda, Peichi, and Natasha. It was Wednesday, the night of the Science Fair. The girls had set their table up in a corner of the gym along with all of the other sixth-grade science projects.

On their table were examples of bread and cake that had risen because yeast or baking powder had been added. They also showed some flatbreads, like matzo, that were made without yeast. Behind their displays was a three-sided project board. It displayed pictures and facts about yeast and fermentation.

"This looks interesting," said one of the judges. "Tell us about it."

Molly stood, as they had planned, and spoke first. Her voice shook as she began. "Yeast is a microorganism that causes a chemical reaction within food," she began. "From earliest times, yeast cells were used to break down the nutrients in cereal grain."

"The byproducts were carbon dioxide and alcohol," Peichi took over. "This process was known as fermentation."

Peichi sat and Natasha stood to say her part. "By four thousand B.C., ancient Egyptians were using fermentation to make beer and wine and also to bake bread. Like beer and wine production, bread baking also depends on the action of yeast cells."

Amanda concluded their talk. "The bread dough contains nutrients that these cells digest. The alcohol that is produced contributes to that wonderful smell of baking bread. The carbon dioxide gas makes the dough rise."

Shawn watched the girls from across the room. Their project looked so good. She picked up the small pulley she had devised for their group. It was made of two empty thread spools hung on metal triangles made from hangers. The spools made up a simple pulley. A rope was wrapped around them and a bucket was attached at the bottom. The idea was that the two spools together made it easier to lift a bucket than lifting it over a single spool. It might have been an okay project, but the wires were taped together badly and didn't hold together. They needed to be retaped at the last minute.

*This project is pathetic*, she thought as she looked at her group's presentation. The judges didn't say much to Shawn when they came by her table. They just made a few marks in their notebook. *We'll probably get a really lousy grade,* Shawn thought. *But this group deserves it.* They had no poster to support their project, only the one-page report that Shawn had written up late the night before. Now she sat at the table alone. Angie and the other girls had immediately run off to hang around at Chris Ratner's table.

Shawn felt like the night dragged on for hours. Finally, though, Molly came by. "You don't seem to be having much fun," she observed.

"Tell me about it," Shawn agreed. "How did you do?"

"We got an honorable mention," Molly told her. "I guess that means we'll get a good grade. We had fun doing it, too. Last night we baked all the cakes and breads. It was crazy! We practically had to hold Amanda back, the cakes smelled so good."

"I should have worked with you guys," Shawn said miserably.

"I'll remind you of that next time a group project comes up," Molly said with a light laugh. "Hey, I have some good news for you."

"What?" Shawn asked.

"Winter break! It starts right now!"

Shawn smiled for the first time all evening. "Way to go!" she cheered.

"Do you want to come out to Pizza Roma with us? We're planning the menu for our New Year's brunch"

"Definitely!" Shawn replied.

125

Amanda awoke as the first gray light of morning streamed into her window. Dressing quickly in jeans and a red sweater, she pulled a box of wrapped gifts from under her bed. She carried it downstairs and put it under the tree in the living room.

Then she knelt at the coffee table and scribbled out a quick note to her family.

Amanda ♥ ♥ ♥ ♥ ♥ ♥ ♥ ♥ ♥ ♥ ♥

HAVE GONE TO THE HOMELESS SHELTER TO HELP NATASHA AND HER FAMILY SERVE BREAKFAST. I WILL BE BACK AS SOON AS I CAN. MERRY CHRISTMAS.

LOVE, AMANDA

P.S. DON'T WAIT FOR ME TO OPEN PRESENTS!

She ran outside and found Natasha and her parents waiting for her.

"We're so glad you're joining us this morning," Mrs. Ross said.

"Well, this is something I really want to do," Amanda said. She smiled at Natasha.

The group walked silently down Eighth Avenue, heading for the big square, brick building that many adults still called the armory. Although the building used to be a place where military supplies were stored, it had been converted into a homeless shelter many years ago.

A light snow began falling and Amanda stuck out her tongue to catch a flake. She glanced at the still-dark windows of all the houses. For a moment, she had the urge to run up to the houses, ring the bells, and shout, "It's snowing! Come on out and see! We're going to have a white Christmas!" But, of course, she knew this was a crazy idea—  something a little kid might do. *I'm not a kid anymore,* she thought. *I've acted like a selfish baby, and it's going to stop.*

When she reached the armory building, she had a sudden desire to run back home. She didn't know what she'd see inside, and it scared her. For a moment, she stood staring at the building, her hands jammed in her pockets.

"Come on in, Amanda," Mr. Ross said. "You don't want to stand out in the snow all day, do you?"

There was no sense being frightened, Amanda told herself. Natasha and her parents did this every year. And she truly wanted to be an unselfish person. This seemed like a good place to start.

Amanda pulled open the heavy door and entered a dark lobby. "This way," Mrs. Ross said. "We'll work on serving the food." Voices and the smell of food came from down the hall to the right. Mrs. Ross held open a swinging door, and they entered a large, well-lit room with many tables.

Amanda followed them over to a long table full of dishes and trays. Other volunteers also stood in a line behind the table. Amanda stood behind a tray of steaming scrambled eggs. Natasha stood next to her, ready to serve blueberry and corn muffins.

Just then, a woman in a lightweight pink coat with ripped pockets got in the line. She had a skinny girl, about four or five years old, with her. The girl's coat didn't have any buttons left on it. They moved down the line, getting pancakes and bacon. "Happy holidays," Natasha said as she used tongs to put a warm blueberry muffin on each of their plates.

"Merry Christmas," Amanda said, scooping eggs onto their plate. She smiled at the little girl. "It's snowing," she told her. "Did you wish for snow this Christmas?"

The girl nodded shyly.

"You made a good wish! Thanks for getting us some snow."

"You're welcome," the girl replied. Her thin, small face suddenly blossomed into a beautiful smile. At that moment, Amanda understood why people said helping others brought them so much joy.

As Amanda continued to serve food, she began thinking about how Dish had started. They'd cooked up food for Justin's family after a fire had ruined their kitchen. They'd felt good about doing that. They'd also been happy when they brought the meals over to Peichi's neighbors. Amanda realized that feeding people really was a way of showing love—and doing it felt great. *Dish should cook more for people who need help*, she thought. *I think I'll bring that up at our next meeting.*

For the next hour, she kept serving eggs. As the time passed she grew more at home in her surroundings. She found it easier to smile and say, "Merry Christmas!" in a strong, cheery voice.

Amanda was scooping up some eggs when Natasha tapped her shoulder. "Look who's here," she said.

Molly, Peichi, and Shawn were crossing the room, coming toward them. Each girl held the gingerbread houses she'd made. "Hey," Molly greeted them. "I saw your note when I woke up and thought this was a great idea. Why didn't you tell me you were going to do this?"

"I didn't know if you'd want to—on Christmas and all," Amanda explained.

"You brought your houses!" Natasha said. "What a great idea!"

Shawn placed her house down on the table. "Yeah. You can't keep these forever, so we figured we might as well put them to use where a lot of people can enjoy them. Believe me, it wasn't easy carrying them over here in the snow!"

Peichi and Molly put their houses on both ends of the table. "That makes it look more jolly," Peichi said.

The woman volunteering to Amanda's left spoke up then. "Would you girls mind taking over for my family and me? We have to drive to our cousins' house in New Jersey and we'd love to get on the road."

"No problem," Peichi said as she reached for a spoon.

"The second shift has arrived," Shawn added.

On the day after Christmas, the Chef Girls sat in the Moores' living room, still planning their New Year's brunch. "I can't believe how much cool cooking stuff Mom and Dad gave us. I have to grill something with my new electric grill. And we'll have to make waffles with the waffle maker," Molly said.

"I think the rotisserie is the best cooking thing we got," Amanda said.

"I have great news," Natasha said. "You guys *really* impressed my parents! They liked you so much at Hanukkah, and they thought it was great the way you came to serve breakfast at Christmas. And Mrs. Moore and my mom had a really nice talk on the phone the other day. Because of all that, they said I can sleep over. This will be my first sleepover ever, in my whole life!"

"Fantastic!" Molly cheered.

"Oh, face it! It was the mandelbrodt that changed their minds," Amanda joked. *Did that sound selfish and egotistical?* she wondered. She decided she wouldn't worry about it. Her plan was to become a better person, not a perfect one, and she'd never have any fun if she was always worrying about doing or saying the perfect thing.

"How would you guys feel if Athena slept over, too? She's a cool girl," Molly asked. "And she likes to cook, too. I know she'd love to help us get everything ready."

"If you're inviting her, could I invite Angie?" Shawn asked.

"No way!" Amanda cried.

"Why do you hate her so much?" Shawn asked. "You've never even given her a chance."

"Yeah, well, if I saw Dracula coming down the street, I wouldn't give *him* a chance, either," Amanda answered. "Angie is *not* sleeping over at my house." Now Amanda didn't care one bit if she was being selfish. Selfish or not—sleeping beside Angie Martinez was more than she could ever stand. And Amanda already knew that she wouldn't have *any* fun at her own party if Angie was there making fun of her for the entire night. Amanda glanced at Shawn's frown. She sighed. "Okay, she can come to brunch, but that's it."

"That's a great idea!" Peichi said. "The sleepover will be for just the five of us. And we'll invite other people to come over for the brunch on New Year's Day."

"I like it," Molly said. She went to the computer and turned it on. "Let's compose our e-mail invitation right now. Who should we invite?"

"Angie," Shawn said.

"Athena," Molly added.

"Tessa," Amanda said. "And Justin! And Connor and Omar."

Molly wrinkled her nose. "*Boys?*" she asked. "Do we have to invite boys?"

"Oh, come on, Molls, it will be fun! Just like cooking class!" Amanda encouraged her.

"Yeah, I think we should!" Shawn agreed. She smiled at Amanda.

"Oh, all right." Molly logged on to the Internet and began typing e-mail addresses. Then she smiled. "This is going to be great!"

Amanda shut off the vacuum cleaner. "I had no idea our room was like a giant dust ball," she said to Molly.

Molly stopped cleaning their full-length mirror. "I know," she agreed. "This mirror is super-smeared. We should make this party an annual thing, so our room will get at least one big cleaning every year!"

"It's going to be so fun. What pajamas are you going to wear?"

"I have no idea," Molly replied. "Listen, Amanda, can I talk to you about something?"

Amanda sat on her bed. "Sure. What?"

"This is the end of the year. I want to start the new year fresh, without any bad feelings."

Amanda was pretty sure she knew what this was going to be about. "I thought you weren't mad at me anymore."

Molly sat down beside her. "I'm not. But I still have one question that's been bothering me. Why did you lie to me about being sick? Didn't you think you could tell me what you wanted to do?"

133

"You would have just said it wasn't fair and there was no way I could leave early."

"Maybe I would have," Molly agreed. "But maybe we could have worked something out. Like, we could have said you could leave early if you cooked extra Dish meals for our next job, or did all the delivery, or something like that."

"You would have really thought that was okay?" Amanda asked.

"I think so," Molly said. "I think I would have done it if you'd explained to me how much you really, really wanted to go. And I would have tried to convince everybody else that it would be okay, too."

"I should have trusted you to be on my side," Amanda realized. "You've always been on my side. It was dumb of me to think you wouldn't be there for me this time."

Molly put her arm around Amanda and the twins hugged.

"Another plate of hot nachos coming up," Molly announced, as she pulled the chili-and-cheese-covered chips from the oven.

Amanda opened the refrigerator. "Don't tell me we're out of soda!" she cried, horrified.

"There's more in our fridge downstairs," Molly told her.

Amanda sighed with relief. "Thank goodness!" She ran down the steps to the basement.

Molly brought the tray into the living room. She set it down on the trivets they'd placed on the coffee table. "Manda's getting more soda," she announced.

"I'm tired of playing Charades," Peichi said. "Let's do something else." She turned on the TV and found the channel that showed the crowd in Times Square. They were all waiting for midnight, when the huge silver ball would drop. "Someday I'm going to go to Manhattan and do that," she said. "It looks like such a blast! It must be the biggest party in the world!"

"Want to play Truth or Dare?" Molly suggested.

"I'm not sure how to play that," Natasha admitted.

"It's easy," Shawn said. "You have to choose if you want to answer a personal question or do a dare. But the tricky part is that you don't know what the question or the dare is ahead of time. It could be a really personal question, or a really embarrassing dare!"

"I don't know," Natasha said. "It doesn't sound like much fun."

"Oh, it is!" Peichi said. "Try it, you'll like it."

"Yeah, it's usually fun, but can we trust Amanda to tell the truth?" Shawn said.

Amanda was walking into the room with soda. She got there just in time to hear Shawn's remark. "I made one mistake and I said I was sorry," she said to Shawn angrily as she put the soda on the table. "When are you going to drop it?"

"You don't have a right to blow up just because I said what I think," Shawn told her.

"I'll say what I think, then," Amanda came back at her. "I'm pretty tired of you treating us like your second-choice friends. You've been ditching Dish ever since you became a cheerleader. You even ditched us on the science project. I thought we were best friends—but then you went and told Angie that I like Justin. I would *never* do that to you!"

"What?" Shawn cried.

"She knew that I like him! She told me so at Connor's party."

"She did *not* get that info from me!" Shawn insisted. "I would never do that! Either someone else told her or she figured it out for herself."

Amanda remembered that she'd been talking to Justin just before Angie spoke to her. Maybe Angie really *had* figured it out on her own.

"I agree with Amanda on one thing. You haven't been hanging with us as much as you used to," Molly said.

Shawn looked uncomfortable. "I love Dish and really want to be a part of it. I love cheerleading, too, though.

It's not easy balancing two groups of friends," she said. "You guys are really different. It's not like I can just get everyone to hang out together. I'm sorry if I've hurt anyone's feelings. I never wanted to."

"I guess it must be hard," Peichi said. "I just wish you'd prefer us to them sometimes."

"I wish I'd done the Science Fair with you," Shawn said.

"You would have had a much better project," Peichi said bluntly.

"I know. Believe me, I know! I'm sorry, guys. I'll try to be around more next year, which is in less than fifteen minutes," Shawn said. "I'll make it my New Year's resolution. And I'll get off your case, Amanda—if you get off mine."

"Deal," Amanda agreed. "My New Year's resolution is never to lie to you guys again."

Natasha cleared her throat anxiously. All the girls looked at her. "As long as we're all telling the truth..." she said.

Molly and Amanda glanced at each other. Was this it? Would she tell them her big secret?

Natasha coughed and looked up at the ceiling. For a moment, they thought she'd changed her mind. But then she bit her lip and began again. "This is something I've been meaning to tell you for a while. I just didn't know how to say it. So...this is the thing...I'm adopted."

Molly caught Amanda's eye and gave a little sigh of relief. Amanda knew how she felt. They'd both imagined that Natasha's problem was much worse than this. She was obviously upset about it. But to them, it hardly seemed like a problem at all.

"I only found out last year," she went on. "I found some papers and asked my parents, and they told me they adopted me when I was a little baby. I've been upset about it ever since I found out."

"What upsets you about being adopted?" Molly asked.

"I don't know...it's not being adopted that upsets me. But not knowing for so many years...it seems like my parents lied to me for my entire life," she replied. "That's one of the reasons I was so mean to you guys last year. I was so jealous. Your lives seemed so easy and your families are so great."

"But we *all* have problems. My mom died. And I miss her every day," Shawn said quietly. Molly reached out and put her arm around her.

"Besides, Natasha, your family is great, too," Amanda said.

"I guess. But I felt like I didn't have a clue who I even was, who my birth family is, what my birth parents even look like. I've felt awful about it. I just have so many questions now. And my adoption is called a closed adoption. That means that the records are sealed so the birth parents can have privacy. So I may never know the answers to all the questions I have." Natasha's eyes brimmed with tears. "And when we met Peichi's neighbors and their little baby, I totally lost it. I'm so sorry I took it all out on you. I've felt awful about it." Tears rolled down her cheeks. Shawn, Peichi, Molly, and Amanda covered her in hugs.

"Hey! Look at the TV!" Peichi exclaimed. They all let go and stared at the screen. The countdown to the new year had begun. Together, they joined in the count: "Five, four, three, two, one...Happy New Year!" Everyone screamed and laughed. Then a light clicked on at the top of the stairs.

"Girls, please keep it down...I don't want Matthew to wake up!" said Mom's quiet voice. Everyone dissolved into giggles. *Quiet* giggles.

"These are too cute!" Shawn said the next day—New Year's Day. They had taken tortillas, moistened them with melted butter, then formed them into baskets. They cut strips of extra tortillas for handles. Then they baked them until they were crispy and filled the baskets with scrambled eggs and bacon.

"They're great, but *this* is what everyone will want,"

Amanda insisted. She'd made a quiche. First she had made dough that was like a pie crust, but not sweet. She'd pressed it carefully into a pie pan as though she were making a regular pie. Then she had mixed up eggs, milk, salt, and pepper. She had poured the egg mixture into the pie shell and sprinkled cooked crumbled bacon and grated cheddar cheese evenly over the top. Finally, Amanda had baked the quiche in the oven for about thirty minutes.

"This waffle maker is the best," said Molly. She poured the batter into it and listened to it sizzle.

Peichi carefully opened the oven door. "Wow!" she exclaimed. "This coffee cake looks so amazing! And it smells *delicious!*"

Natasha was busy setting up the table. She carried orange juice, maple syrup, boysenberry syrup, powdered sugar, salt and pepper, and a basket of warm cinnamon rolls into the dining room.

Amanda ran upstairs and put on her short skirt with the new boots she'd finally gotten for Christmas. Knowing Justin would be there, she gave her hair a few waves with the curling iron. Maybe she could erase his memory of the way she'd looked at the gingerbread house class.

By eleven o'clock their guests began to arrive. Omar

and Connor showed up first. "We're starving," Omar said. "Look at all that food! Let me at it!"

"His New Year's resolution is to gain a hundred pounds this year!" Connor teased as he came in behind Omar.

Justin and Athena were the next to come. Then Tessa arrived, followed by Angie. The Moores' dining room was soon full of delicious smells and lots of laughter.

"Matthew, stay away from the pastries!" Molly scolded her brother. He was attempting to eat his fourth cinnamon roll. With an impish grin, he grabbed it and darted out of the room.

"Who made this freaky egg pie?" Angie asked.

 "Amanda did," Shawn told her. "It's called quiche. And, actually, I think it's cool. I'm going to try some." She took a slice and ate a bite. "Wow! It's great."

"If you say so," Angie said. "It's too weird-looking for me."

Amanda smiled at Shawn. They exchanged a happy thumbs-up.

"Hey, Amanda." She turned and faced Justin. "This food is so *good!* You guys did a great job."

She smiled at him. "I'm glad you came."

"It's funny," he said. "Did you know that I always felt a little odd around you?"

"You did? Why?" Amanda asked.

"I don't know," he admitted. "You always looked so

neat and perfect. But when I saw you in your old clothes at the gingerbread class, I realized you were just a regular person, like me."

"Yup, just a regular person," Amanda said. Wow! He liked her as she really was. She had always gone to so much trouble to look good for him—and he liked her best when she looked her worst.

"Excuse me," she said to him. "We're out of orange juice. I need to run downstairs and get some more."

Molly watched her sister leave Justin and pick up the empty punch bowl. She'd actually left her major crush to pitch in and do her share of the work.

What a change!

Molly smiled. She had a feeling that the coming year would bring lots of changes—good, exciting changes. And it really *would* be a happy New Year.

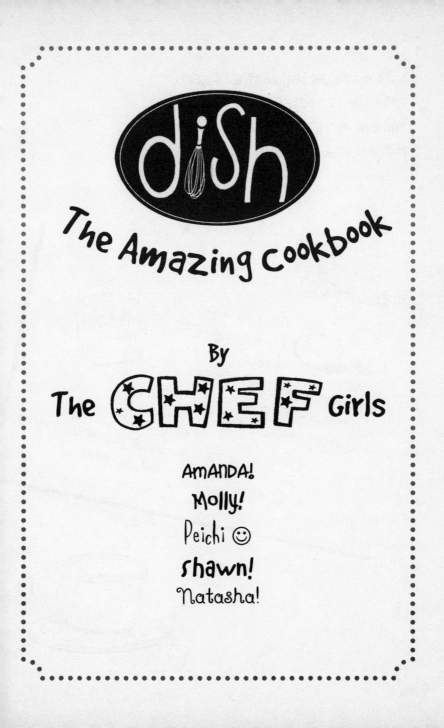

# dish

## The Amazing Cookbook

### By

## The CHEF Girls

AMANDA!

MOLLY!

Peichi ☺

shawn!

Natasha!

THIS MANDELBRODT RECIPE IS REALLY
EASY AND IT TASTES REALLY DELICIOUS.
YOU CAN ADD EITHER NUTS OR CHOCOLATE
CHIPS—I LIKE CHOCOLATE CHIPS THE BEST!

—AMANDA

# MANDELBRODT

1 1/2 CUPS SUGAR

3/4 CUP SHORTENING

3 EGGS

2 TEASPOONS VANILLA EXTRACT

3 CUPS FLOUR

1 TEASPOON BAKING POWDER

DASH OF SALT

4 OUNCES OF CHOPPED NUTS OR
CHOCOLATE CHIPS

SUGAR
granulated
5 LBS.

1. PREHEAT OVEN TO 350 DEGREES.

2. MIX TOGETHER THE SUGAR AND THE SHORTENING UNTIL THEY'RE COMBINED.

3. BREAK EGGS INTO A BOWL, AND BEAT THEM LIGHTLY.

4. ADD EGGS TO THE SUGAR/SHORTENING MIX AND STIR TOGETHER.

5. ADD VANILLA.

6. NOW STIR IN THE FLOUR, BAKING POWDER, AND SALT. ADD THE NUTS OR CHOCOLATE CHIPS.

7. NOW FORM THE DOUGH INTO FOUR ROLLS (THEY MIGHT LOOK LIKE LOGS) AND PLACE ON A COOKIE SHEET.

8. BAKE 20 TO 25 MINUTES, OR UNTIL GOLDEN BROWN.

9. WAIT UNTIL THE ROLLS/LOGS AREN'T STEAMING HOT (THEY SHOULD STILL BE WARM), AND THEN SLICE THEM INTO 1 INCH SLICES.

# Hummus

1 15-ounce can of chickpeas
(Chickpeas are also called garbanzo beans.)
2 garlic cloves
1/2 lemon
1 teaspoon salt
1 tablespoon tahini
(Tahini is a puree of sesame seeds.
It comes in a can or a jar.)
1/4 to 1/2 cup of water

Rinse and
drain the chickpeas.
Mince the garlic. Squeeze
the juice out of the lemon half.
Put the chickpeas into the food
processor or blender along with the lemon
juice, garlic, salt, and tahini. Turn the
food processor or blender on and
let it run until the chickpeas
are mashed up. Scrape the
mixture off the sides of

the food processor. Slowly add the water—a little bit at a time!—until the hummus looks thick and creamy. Don't add too much—you don't want to make chickpea soup! When you've finished adding the water, let the food processor or blender run for about five minutes. That way, the ingredients will be combined really well and it will taste great! Serve with pita bread, tortilla chips, or sliced raw vegetables such as carrots, celery, tomatoes, and peppers.

My mom taught me how to make hummus—it's really easy! And yummy, too. My mom makes it in a food processor, which makes the hummus really smooth. But you can also use a blender—your hummus will be a little more chunky, but it will still taste great!

—Natasha

# Marinated Portobello Mushrooms over Fresh Pasta

We all love this—even Matthew, who normally won't eat mushrooms! portobello mushrooms are big, brown mushrooms with a lot of flavor. If you don't have fresh pasta, you can serve this over regular pasta and it will still taste really good!

1 shallot
4 cloves of garlic
1 cup extra virgin olive oil
1/3 cup balsamic vinegar
1 teaspoon salt
1 pound of portobello mushrooms

1 pound of fresh pasta (we like to use linguine)
salt and pepper to taste

Mince the shallot and put the garlic through a garlic press. Combine the olive oil, the balsamic vinegar, the pressed garlic, the minced shallot, and the salt in a shallow glass dish. Wash the mushrooms and gently pat them dry. Cut the mushrooms into half-inch slices, and then cut the slices into chunks. Put the mushroom chunks into the glass dish of marinade and stir well so that the mushrooms are completely coated with the marinade. Cover the dish and let it sit in the refrigerator for at least thirty minutes.

Using a slotted spoon, remove the mushroom pieces from the marinade and add them to the skillet (don't add the extra marinade to the pan). Stir the mushrooms constantly over a medium heat until they are browned on all sides.

Add cold water and a pinch of salt to a large pot. Bring the water to a boil over medium-high heat and cook the pasta according to the package directions (if you are using fresh pasta, it will cook very quickly). Drain the pasta and then toss it with the mushrooms. Add half of the remaining marinade to the pasta and stir until the pasta is coated and discard the other half. Add salt and pepper to taste. If you want, you can garnish the pasta with fresh parsley. It will look really pretty!

# cooking tips from the chef Girls!

The Chef Girls are looking out for you!
Here are some things you should
know if you want to cook.
(Remember to ask your parents
if you can use knives and the stove!)

1   Tie back long hair so that it won't
    get into the food or in the way as
    you work.

2   Don't wear loose-fitting clothing
    that could drag in the food or
    on the stove burners.

3   Never cook in bare feet or open-toed
    shoes. Something sharp or hot could
    drop on your feet.

4   Always wash your hands before you
    handle food.

5   Read through the recipe before you start. Gather your ingredients together and measure them before you begin.

6   Turn pot handles in so that they won't get knocked off the stove.

7   Use wooden spoons to stir hot liquids. Metal spoons can become very hot.

8   When cutting or peeling food, cut away from your hands.

9   Cut food on a cutting board, not the countertop.

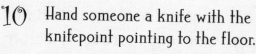

10   Hand someone a knife with the knifepoint pointing to the floor.

11   Clean up as you go. It's safer and neater.

12   Always use a dry pot holder to remove something hot from the oven. You could get burned with a wet one, since wet ones retain heat.

13   Make sure that any spills on the floor are cleaned up right away, so that you don't slip and fall.

14 Don't put knives in clean-up water. You could reach into the water and cut yourself.

15 Use a wire rack to cool hot baking dishes to avoid scorch marks on the countertop.

# An Important Message from the Chef Girls!

Some foods can carry bacteria, such as salmonella, that can make you sick. To avoid salmonella, always cook poultry, ground beef, and eggs thoroughly before eating. Don't eat or drink foods containing raw eggs. And wash hands, kitchen work surfaces, and utensils with soap and water immediately after they have been in contact with raw meat or poultry.

**mooretimes2:** Molly and Amanda

**qtpie490:** Shawn

**happyface:** Peichi

**BrooklynNatasha:** Natasha

**JustMac:** Justin

**Wuzzup:** What's up?

**Mwa** smooching sound

**G2G:** Got To Go

**deets:** details

**b-b:** Bye-Bye

**brb:** be right back

**<3** hearts

**L8R:** Later, as in "See ya later!"

**LOL:** Laughing Out Loud

**GMTA:** Great Minds Think Alike

**j/k:** Just kidding

**B/C:** because

**W8:** Wait

**W8 4 me @:** Wait for me at

**thanx:** thanks

**BK:** Big kiss

**MAY:** Mad about you

**RUF2T?:** Are you free to talk?

**TTUL:** Type to you later

**E-ya:** will e-mail you

**LMK:** Let me know

**GR8:** Great

**WFM:** Works for me

**2:** to, too, two

**C:** see

**u:** you

**2morrow:** tomorrow

**VH:** virtual hug

**BFFL:** Best Friends For Life

**:-@** shock

**:-P** sticking out tongue

**%-)** confused

**:-o** surprised

**;-)** winking or teasing